SNOWFLAKES
AND
COFFEE CAKES

ALSO BY JOANNE DEMAIO

The Winter Novels
Snowflakes and Coffee Cakes
Snow Deer and Cocoa Cheer
Cardinal Cabin
First Flurries
Eighteen Winters
—And More Winter Novels—

The Seaside Saga
Blue Jeans and Coffee Beans
The Denim Blue Sea
Beach Blues
Beach Breeze
The Beach Inn
Beach Bliss
Castaway Cottage
Night Beach
Little Beach Bungalow
Every Summer
Salt Air Secrets
Stony Point Summer
—And More Seaside Saga Books—

Summer Standalone Novels
True Blend
Whole Latte Life

Novella
The Beach Cottage

Snowflakes and Coffee Cakes

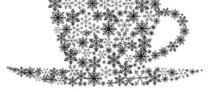

A NOVEL

JOANNE DEMAIO

Copyright © 2013 Joanne DeMaio
All rights reserved.

ISBN: 1492933171
ISBN-13: 978-1492933175

Joannedemaio.com

For Jena, always

one

I<small>F VERA COULD CAPTURE THE</small> perfect image of the long weekend ahead, this would be it, the snowfall a delicate backdrop to her sister standing near the bridal shop window. Even though it's February, this moment feels a little like Christmas Eve, with its quiet anticipation of a special celebration. Her sister wears a vintage satin-and-lace gown with three-quarter lace sleeves for her winter wedding.

"Even the lace looks like a snowflake pattern," Vera says.

Brooke holds out her arms, running a hand lightly over the intricately stitched sleeve. "I hope it snows Saturday. Just a little, like it is now."

"Me, too. Peaceful, wedding-white snow."

The shopkeeper emerges from the back room carrying a package wrapped in tissue. "Here it is," Amy tells them, setting it on the counter and unwrapping the thin paper. "Close your eyes, Brooke."

Brooke steps up on the raised pedestal and squeezes her eyes shut while Vera moves closer to Amy to see. Her sister's gown is so elegant, she can't imagine what more Amy has found for it. That is, not until she lifts out the off-white lace belt embellished with the palest blue-and-ivory satin snowflake, anchored with a silver crystal brooch in its center.

"It's just gorgeous," Vera whispers. "Where did you ever find it?"

"At a flea market in New Hampshire, actually. I went with my mom," Amy says. "And when I saw this, I knew it was meant for Brooke."

"Can I look?" Brooke asks.

"No," they call out in unison while walking over to the pedestal with it.

"May I?" Vera asks, and Amy gives her the belt. Carefully she reaches around her sister's waist, her hands skimming the satin, and secures it in place. A small adjustment to the sparkling snowflake precisely centers the belt on the gown. Vera steps back then, her eyes welling as the reality of her sister's winter wedding sinks in with the reflection of the two of them, side by side, Brooke in white, Vera in a blue velvet dress.

"Okay, open," Vera whispers. It's all she can manage, really, without breaking out in true honest-to-goodness crying.

Brooke opens her eyes and when Amy sets the birdcage veil over her brown hair pulled back in a loose chignon, Brooke's eyes move from the snowflake sash up to Vera's in the reflection. "Do you like it?" she asks.

"Like it? I absolutely love it," Vera says.

"Me, too. But you looked a little sad there for a second."

Vera steps up on the pedestal and gives her sister a hug. "Those are just tears," she assures her. "Happy tears.

2

You will be *thee* most beautiful bride Saturday."

And all the while Vera tries to convince herself that tears are tears, right? Don't all tears look the same, happy or sad? They're nothing more than a bit of moisture that, according to her father, eventually contributes to water vapor and finds its way to a snowflake. At least she has the excuse of her sister's wedding to blame on these tears. Because now is so not the time to tell her family that for all Brooke's happiness, she's just lost her job. Gotten one of the many pink slips circulating through the newspaper business these days. She'd never believed she'd be on the receiving end, not after writing four years of news articles, advancing each year to more serious and prominent pieces. The shock of it continues to bring up those darn tears as she steps off the pedestal.

"Vera?" Brooke asks.

Vera looks over at her, silently, lest an *I'm unemployed and afraid* sob escapes.

"I *really* missed you," her sister says, "and am so happy you're home."

Home, home, home. Having been away from it makes Vera realize how many things it can be: their old house, her childhood town, a holiday memory. It can be merely a sense of security. How much of her nostalgia this snowy day is only that, a longing for everything home. All she can manage is to give her sister the assuring smile she is waiting for.

"I wish you didn't have to go back to Boston." Brooke reaches over and brushes a piece of lint from the blue velvet maid-of-honor dress Vera is wearing.

"What do you do in the city?" Amy asks as she fans out the wedding gown's chapel train behind Brooke.

Vera pauses, unwilling to reveal just yet that she's been

laid off. "I'm a journalist for the paper there."

"Oh, now that's exciting. What do you write about?"

"Lately it's been the local angle on national stories. But if I were writing this weekend, it would definitely be for the society page, covering one very special wedding. Speaking of which, I think Dad's waiting at home, Brooke."

"I'll get these dresses wrapped up so the snow doesn't get on them," Amy says, still fussing with the gown. "And what's next on the pre-wedding agenda?"

"We're building a snowman," Brooke tells her, twisting to look at her gown train in the full-length mirror.

"A snowman?"

Vera helps Brooke take off the lace sash. "What happens when your father is Leo Sterling, the local meteorologist with a passion for winter, is that you know things like this: Every ten minutes," Vera begins, glancing at Amy, "the earth's atmosphere produces enough snow to build a snowman for each person on the planet."

"Seriously?" Amy takes the sash from Vera.

"Oh, yes. And our dad works really hard to keep up with those numbers, building a snowman in our front yard for every occasion, every holiday, every event he can think of. So we're building a wedding snowman today, to greet our guests this weekend."

"My daughter, Grace, built her very first snowman last week," Amy tells them.

"That's so sweet!" Brooke says. "How old is your daughter?"

"Two, the perfect age for snow play. And I have a great idea, hang on a sec." Amy rushes into her back room and Vera hears her rustling through things before emerging with an old satin top hat. "Please take this. It's my contribution to your snowman collection. Because as

4

Addison's official wedding authority, I declare that you cannot display a wedding snowman without the right, jaunty finishing touch."

Dreams do come true. Brooke kept her guest list to under seventy-five for an intimate affair, and transformed Addison's community center sparse hall into a winter wonderland. Yes, two days later, Vera sees every childhood wedding dream her sister ever imagined come to life. Silver spray-painted branches reach from centerpiece vases; white feathers gently sway in Brooke's white rose bouquet; silver and blue glass balls and crystal snowflakes sparkle in clear decorative bowls, the snowflake motif continuing in a glittering garland strung around each white table. Even the wedding cake was dreamt up by Brooke. She made her own Tiffany-blue-frosted chocolate cake, its center filled with a white-icing heart. Because for Brooke, love is in the air *and* in the cake. Or muffins. Or brownies. Anything she bakes comes with love. And so Vera's thrilled that her dear sister's winter wedding is going off without a hitch.

It's her own hitches that worry her, the ones that come from aunts and cousins she hasn't seen in years. All evening, prying questions spin around her like snow swirling from the clouds: *When are you getting married, Vera? Maybe you'll have a wedding just like your sister's. How's the job in the city? Are you dating anyone there? Your mother says you're seeing someone you work with. Is he here? Can we meet him? Maybe he's the one!*

It's all she can do to politely nod and politely lie until Brooke, as always, senses her distress and swoops in for the rescue, her lace-and-satin gown shimmering behind her.

"Come on, sis." She grabs Vera's arm and tugs her to the dance floor. "I requested your favorite dance."

"Wait! Brooke, I'm really—"

"One, two, three, *go!*" the DJ suddenly announces as the Electric Slide begins and a crowd of people lines the dance floor, fanning out around Brooke and her winter-white gown. "Step right, left, behind," the DJ calls for anyone unsure of the moves. "Right, tap, clap."

Seeing no way out, and maybe glad for it too, Vera falls easily into step in her blue velvet dress, kicking and sliding further away from inquisitive relatives with each beat of the song.

"Bend forward, bring it down, bring it down," the DJ calls, and what Vera sees is that the wedding guests don't really need instruction. She figures most of them have spent plenty of Thursdays at Joel's Bar on line-dancing night. Which is yet another thing she realizes she misses from home, now that she is home: all the local hangouts and the local get-togethers.

"That's right, keep it going now."

And the guests do, sliding and stomping across the floor.

If only Vera could keep her life going as easy as that, just scoot, step and tap through her days. Old friends around her wear glimmering dresses and the very best suits for her newlywed sister and brother-in-law. She's not sure if she's seen a happier couple than Brooke and Brett. But seriously? The way Brooke feeds him, it's no wonder he's always smiling.

"Hey," a dancing guest says, touching her arm. "Vera?"

Vera looks over at him for a second. "Greg?"

"Bring it back, bring it back, bring it back," the DJ chants.

"Good to see you, Vera," he says, stepping close beside her. "It's been a long time."

"And turn around," the DJ adds.

When she spins and looks up, it's not Greg at her side, but another familiar face. One she can't place, though. He catches her eye, too, in his vest and button-down shirt, the sleeves cuffed, going through the slide motions with ease.

"Okay ladies and gentlemen, it's time to put your hands together, this time in each *other's* arms, as we move and groove right into a slow number now."

At the same time the guy with the familiar face takes her left elbow, Greg takes her right arm, unaware of the other dancer.

"So where have you been keeping yourself, Vera?" he asks. "Because you are truly a sight for sore eyes."

"Greg, hey," she says with a smile, glancing quickly over her shoulder at the face of the other man who wanted only a dance, only with her. A few minutes of closeness, of questions, of touch. His dark brown hair curls over his collar and as he moves away, his face is shadowed, whether by the dim lighting or by life she isn't sure.

"Can't stay away from Addison, can you? I heard you were back in town," Greg says.

"Just for a few days. Because as much as I love visiting, you know how it is. Life calls, and mine calls me back to Boston."

"Word on the street is that you're a big-time reporter now."

"Oh I'm not sure how big-time it is, but you know.

I'm doing what I love, chasing the news stories." She feels his hand on her shoulder turning her into the dance, the folds of her blue velvet dress swinging with the steps. "How about you, Greg? What have you been up to? Do you still live in town?"

"Moved back after college and have been here since." He leads her into another turn. "I keep busy, my folks are around, my brother's here."

She waves her fingers at her mother and father twirling past beside her. "You're lucky, being near family," Vera tells him as she watches them dance, her mother's pleated gown fanning out in a spin.

"Lucky? Maybe sometimes. Other times it feels like just more of the job. You know, if I'm not fixing things at home, or with the family, I'm fixing things all day long at work."

Vera tries to remember what he does, certain her sister had mentioned it in the past few days. When they make another turn, she notices the mystery dancer putting on his jacket, getting ready to leave. He catches her eye and if she's not mistaken, hitches his head slightly at her as he goes. She glances back at him again, still unable to place his familiar face.

"Lord knows there's always something at work needing fixing," Greg is saying.

Vera looks back at him right as the bouquet-toss announcement is made. She thanks Greg for the dance as a cousin tugs her toward the bouquet-crowd. Can it be that time already? Where did the night go? So much of life's been like that, passing by unnoticed until it is suddenly gone. Her job, a visit home, Brooke's wedding. A dance, a few words, a look. Passing as quickly as that one moment on the dance floor, the moment a man took her elbow for two seconds that never amounted to more than that, yet linger still.

The snowman stands with his top hat tipped at the same saucy angle, but today, the sauciness seems gone. If Vera's not mistaken, she thinks he looks a little forlorn, wanting the happy time of the weekend back. And the snow hasn't stopped, either, more arriving the day after Brooke's wedding, the day Vera heads back north. Her parents' gray colonial is dusted in fresh white powder, the windows glowing with lamplight, her mother holding aside the lace curtain and watching her pull out of the driveway. And she knows. Home can be a big, boisterous family or a shadow of what once was. Because her memory of the weekend, which is only a shadow of it now, will always *feel* like home. Her heart tells her so. As she puts the car in gear on the street, Vera gives a small wave to the snowman, then presses a finger to her eye to stem the tears.

So her younger sister is married now. She'll settle into life right here in town, where her husband is an accountant, keeping the numbers of their lives straight and orderly. And her parents' nest is empty now, too, so there's that. As happy as weekends like this are, there's always a sadness about them, because with the significant marking of chapters opening there always comes a chapter closing.

While driving through Addison, crossing the train tracks toward the historical part of town to pick up the highway there, the snow continues falling. Vera leans forward to see the view clearly on the return trip to

Boston. Returning to what, though, she's not sure. Well. She is sure—sure that it's nothing. It's a life for which there is little more than this imagined headline: Unemployed and Single. The rest is yet to be written. It's ironic that as a journalist she writes everyone else's story, but doesn't even know her own.

The wind outside blows whispers of snow around old neighborhood landmarks: Whole Latte Life Coffee Café looking cozy with its frosted, illuminated windowpanes; the vintage bridal shop Wedding Wishes with twinkly lights around the doorway; the local nursery with snowy garden statues holding still until spring; The Green and its grand wishing fountain … all on a Main Street lined with historical Cape Cods and saltbox colonials. Why she ever decided to leave this picturesque snow-globe town is sometimes beyond her.

The snow falls even heavier. For all her father taught her about winter and snowflakes, still, in a magical and sad moment like this, as she sees her old hometown through a windshield covered with glistening crystals, she has to wonder: What are snowflakes, really? Today she'd say they're nothing more than perfect stars dropped down to earth, each one a treasure, casting a sense of hope on the view through her window.

Winter stars. But do snowy winter stars possess the same power as celestial stars up above? If she could wish on a winter star right now, pick the biggest star-shaped white glittering snowflake that she could find and make a wish, what would it be? To not leave behind her family? To find a new journalism job, soon? To have someone in her life? Or to just embrace *whatever* comes her way, like the way she's embracing the swirling snow tumbling down on this little town.

A few blocks before picking up the highway, as she nears the cove, Vera squints through that darn snowy windshield and turns the wipers on faster to make out the approaching view. The street is lined with tall old maple trees, the white snow like gloves on the branches reaching skyward. Those gloved branches frame historic homes with gingerbread trim and gabled roofs and wraparound post-and-rail front porches, some of the homes behind white picket fences.

The snow is falling so thickly, crystals and dendrites and ice particles at once, that one Dutch colonial, the last home on the street, seems to rise from it all like a dream.

Or a wish, she thinks, as she looks at it wistfully. Set off to the side behind the old house is a large barn, looking merely like a shadow hulking behind the white snowfall. Its snow-covered roof and brown weathered wood planks bring back wintry childhood memories from when it was the Christmas Barn, full of wonder year-round. And there's one more thing she notices as her car crawls along, as her arms pull her even closer to the windshield to squint through the swishing wipers growing more coated with wet snow with each passing second. A faded FOR SALE sign stands in the front yard, a little crooked and nearly buried in the winter's snow, as though it's been there for a long time.

Vera lifts her foot off the gas and slams on the brakes, not that she really has to; she was driving so slowly already while mesmerized by the enchanted view. Beyond the imposing dark barn, Addison Cove stretches out, its crystal-blue waters frozen solid and covered with a blanket of white as it winds its way to the Connecticut River.

She parks in front of the house, gets out of her car and

walks through the freshly fallen snow, slipping a little on the walkway, just to take a peek inside. Just to see if it all still looks like it did years ago when her parents brought her to the Christmas Barn. Ending the weekend with a drive down memory lane feels right, somehow. Oh, if ever she'd wish for a beautiful home of her own, wouldn't this be it? Vera stamps her snow-caked boots on the Dutch colonial's front stoop and leans over to the side, trying to glimpse into the vacant house through the dusty paned windows, tightening her scarf against the blowing snow swirls, glancing up at those winter stars falling around her and closing her eyes tightly, for a long second, feeling the crystal snowflakes land on her face.

two

Seven Months Later – September

WHAT WAS SHE THINKING? WELL. Vera knows *what* she was thinking. Something along the lines of visions of grandeur being easily attained. All it takes is talking yourself into buying a moss-green, wood-sided, run-down New England colonial with a widow's walk, no less, and a rambling barn too, and life will be as magnificent as the house. That the home was historic, once owned by a seafaring ship captain, even better.

It seemed like a good idea at the time. After watching the status of the unsold property online for months, and the status of her uneventful employment search, Vera finally decided. Before frittering away the sizable severance pay that came with her pink slip, that money needed to be invested. In real estate. In one particular piece of Addison, Connecticut real estate, right beside the cove. Invested in drafty windows, in creaky floorboards, in a loose shutter, and in peeling paint.

And right up until Vera stained the Dutch colonial's

heavy front door a dark barnwood brown to match the brown timber barn that is *also* now hers, the idea still seemed good. She even sanded and stained the antique scrolled pediment above the door. A little painting, a little cleaning, a little patching, and the house was … home.

And still is, even as she hooks a hammer claw around a large nail in the living room wall and yanks. Oh sure, yanks half a wall of Sheetrock with the effort, veins and threaded cracks instantly spreading across the surface.

"Swell," she says, stepping back and gauging the damage. "Now what?" Okay, so there has to be some way to fix this, because everything can be fixed, right? She just needs someone to tell her how. At least on the way to the hardware store, Vera gets to walk outside through her newly stained front door, looking back over her shoulder with, well, with hope at least.

❦

"Read me back the order," Derek says into the phone. He leans an elbow on the countertop, checking off items on the list as his vendor repeats the order he just placed: snow shovels, windshield scrapers, roof rakes, snow-melt, sidewalk scrapers and electric snow throwers. "Throw in an extra carton of the windshield scrapers, would you? I have a feeling we're in for a good winter."

"What are you looking for in a delivery date? First week of October?" the vendor asks.

"If not sooner. I always get those early-bird shoppers preparing for the worst. You know how that goes."

"I'll do my best. We're getting busy. Can't believe the holidays are right around the corner, Derek. Where'd the year go?"

Twelve months. Where they went, he can't say for certain. Doesn't really matter, though. Because no matter how much you'd like to, there's no getting any of it back once it's gone, not one damn minute. Not one lousy day. Not one split-second decision. He pulls off his baseball cap, runs a hand through his hair and resettles the cap backward on his head, then cuffs his sleeve and checks his watch before giving his wrist a quick shake. Day after day, still, his eye is drawn to his watch every midafternoon with the habitual time check, except when he gets busy enough to be distracted from thinking about it.

He turns to the wall calendar behind the hardware store counter and lifts the September page to October to verify his order's delivery date. As he raises up this month's page to the October weeks not far off, his eye goes to the thick layer of tape plastered over and again along the top of the calendar where the hook passes through. Then he rips the whole damn thing right off the wall hook and throws it all in the trash can at his feet.

Late-afternoon sunbeams reach through the paned windows. She loves the way that happens, the way the sun's golden color heralds the approach of fall. That and the creaking wood floors of Cooper Hardware have to be two of her favorite things. Vera walks along the aisle looking up and down the racks of Spackle and Sheetrock tape and spackling knives. She can do this, she knows she can. But it would be a lot easier if there were some manual to guide her.

"Can I help you?"

She looks up at an older man approaching. "I hope so.

I've got a wall that needs repairing and if you could maybe walk me through the process, I think I'll do okay."

"What kind of wall are we talking about?"

Vera looks from his eyes to the shelves. "Sheetrock? I bought an old house here in town and I'm doing a few repairs."

"Is that right. Now which house is it? Because if it's old enough, the walls might be plaster."

"Plaster? Hmm. It's the green colonial at the cove. Where the Christmas Barn used to be?"

"No kidding. The big Dutch?"

"Yes, the last one on the street. With the barn too, it looks right out on the water there."

"I know exactly the house you're talking about. Have you moved in yet?"

"I did, about a month ago now. And I was fixing things up until a wall and I didn't get along too well this morning, so what started as patching a nail hole is now a major repair." She shrugs a little. "Help?"

"My son's the carpenter. Derek. He does small renovations and repairs on the side. Why don't you have a talk with him and see what he can do?"

"And where would I find him?"

The man points to the rear of the store near the office. "Right back there, doing some paperwork."

Vera glances quickly over, then thanks him before heading down the aisle.

"Oh, Miss! Watch out for Zeus," the man calls after her.

"Zeus?" she asks, turning back while still walking slowly, a little confused.

He motions with his arm raised, his finger pointing downward and to the left, so she stops suddenly and looks in front of her. A big yellow lab is spread sound-asleep across the wood-planked floor in a patch of afternoon sunlight. "Zeus?" she asks, and the man nods at her before walking away.

"Seems like you've got the right idea," she says to the dog while stepping over him and rounding the corner to the rear aisle, just in time to see this Derek ripping a calendar off the wall and throwing it, not too casually either, in the trash.

"Excuse me," she calls out and he looks up at her. So she takes a few steps closer. "Your dad sent me your way?"

He lifts off his cap and resettles it over his dark tousled hair, adding a quick glance at the now calendar-less wall. "What can I do for you?"

Vera hesitates, feeling as though she's interrupted something, though he's alone at the counter. She takes a quick breath and extends her hand. "I'm Vera. Vera Sterling."

He shakes her hand briefly. "Derek Cooper."

"Cooper, so your family owns the store?" She looks at him for a second longer, taking in his tall frame, a shadow of whiskers and brown eyes. "Do I know you from somewhere?"

He shakes his head and shrugs. "You from around here?"

"I am. Well, I was. I recently moved back. Do you have a sister by any chance?"

"Samantha."

"Really! I went to school with Sam. Sam Cooper. How is she?"

"She's good. Manages the store here, keeps me and my Dad in line. Married a couple years now."

"Wow. I haven't seen her in ages."

"Where'd you move to?"

"I'm sorry?"

"You said you moved back here. In town?"

"Yes, yes I did. And I'm doing some home repairs, trying to make a grand dream come true with a handyman's special, if you get my drift. Which now has wall damage I need fixed up. Your father said you do small repairs on the side?"

"I can take a look at it. What's the address?"

"Oh you can't miss it. It's the last house down at the cove, the one with the barn."

"The old Christmas Barn?"

"That's the one. So you know it?"

He looks past her for a second, quiet. "Yeah, I do."

And that's all he says, glancing down at the trash can where he'd thrown that calendar, adjusting the cap on his head, then sliding a pencil and paper across the counter. "Write down your name and phone number. I'll try to stop by the next day or two."

She takes the pencil. "I know it's short notice, but I'm sure I can find someone else if you're busy."

"No." He folds down his black denim shirt cuff, then recuffs it. "No, it's not a problem." He checks his watch.

"Well. Okay, then." Vera jots down the information and slides it back to him. "Thanks. You'll call first?"

When he only nods and puts her number in a pocket of his cargo pants, she turns to leave. But she turns back, looking at him for a moment more before adding, "Say hi to Samantha for me?" He nods again, and so she heads out, giving a quick glance over her shoulder to see him lifting that creased and taped-up wall calendar carefully out of the trash.

three

A BALLERINA STANDS IN CLASSIC pirouette form, her pale gold tutu the color of late September's maple tree leaves. "I can't believe you still don't have a job," Brooke says while leaning over and lifting the scarecrow's bent arm a little higher, then tucking loose straw into its ballet slipper.

Vera pulls her cropped tweed jacket close with a glance at her ripped jeans. "If you're referring to my pants, the rips are intentional, Brooke. They're not because I don't have any money. Distressed denim is actually in."

Brooke looks her up and down. "Seriously, Vee." They pass a podium in front of the historical society building and each take a ballot to rate the scarecrows. Brooke tucks hers in her denim jacket pocket as they cross the street. "Let's stop on The Green, I brought us something to eat."

They settle on a garden bench with their pumpkin spice lattes to-go and Brooke reaches into a large tote, her French braid falling over her shoulder. She pulls out a plastic tray of mini cinnamon-crumb coffee cakes.

"Employed or not, I can count on you to keep me fed,

regardless," Vera says as she peels the lid off her coffee.

Brooke hands her two cakes and a napkin. "I just don't get what you're doing, Vera. You need a job, and fast now. It's been so long since you had a paycheck come in."

"No kidding," Vera says around a mouthful of the coffee cake. "And you'll be happy to know money *is* on its way because I've lined up freelance assignments with the *Addison Weekly*." She nudges her sister's arm, pointing to the medical building nearby. A scarecrow doctor clad in a white jacket holds a stethoscope to a worried-looking patient, her straw hair standing on end. "One of which is a profile of the Annual Scarecrow Competition."

"Really? You've gone from Boston news to Addison scarecrows? I don't know, Vera. The longer you're away from journalism, the more out of touch you'll be with the field. I'm worried about you."

"Well I'll get paid for this piece, so don't worry too much."

"Come on, how much can they pay you? You're kind of slumming it a little. Because there's no way freelancing for the town newspaper will cover your bills."

"I've got a few leads I'm following up on. And I was thinking of renting out my barn. Lots of people need that kind of storage space, so it'll help until a story breaks."

"The barn, the house. I'm sorry, but it's all kind of a dump and it seems like you're in way over your head. I still don't understand why you want to renovate instead of move into a nice townhouse, maybe?"

Vera sips her hot coffee, letting her sister ramble while talking with her hands, a turquoise-ringed finger hammering home a point. Vera stopped listening somewhere around townhouse. Because she's done the whole condo thing already. And really, what does Brooke know about being single and unemployed, when you'll take any comfort you can find, even if it's only in the *hope* of what can be? Her vision of her big colonial dream home hasn't wavered, even though her checkbook is beginning to.

"Tell me you're at least thinking of flipping that house to help pay off your college loans." Brooke stands and they cross to Main Street, stopping in front of the elementary school to rate the teacher scarecrow writing at a portable chalkboard. "Did you ever think about teaching?" Brooke asks as she rates the school display on her ballot. "Like maybe a journalism class at the community college?"

Vera considers the teacher scarecrow with a bandana around its neck and a couple old-fashioned wooden desks set out behind her. "Two stars to your suggestion. And four to the display," she says as she notes her voting ballot.

They walk on in the late-September sunlight, approaching a New York Yankees batter facing off a Boston Red Sox pitcher, the mini-stadium set up in front of Joel's Bar and Grille. The Yankee player's arms are overstuffed with straw, ready to hit the ball out of the park. Vera lifts her sunglasses on top of her head. "Oh now this one is fun. There's definitely going to be a rivalry in the votes here." She discreetly notes her five-star Yankee rating with a *Go Yankees* addendum.

"Hey look, it's me and Brett." Brooke nudges Vera's arm as they near Wedding Wishes. Bride and groom scarecrows stand side by side in the afternoon sunlight, the bride wearing a pleated cream gown and a birdcage veil similar to the one Brooke wore. Satin gloves are tucked on the end of the bride's straw arms. They see Amy through the shop window and give her display a thumbs-up, and when her young daughter steps close to the door to watch them, they send along a happy wave to her, too.

But rating scarecrow astronauts, and a fireman climbing a ladder to a stuffed cat on a branch, and a police officer writing a ticket, merely fuels Brooke's job ideas. "Maybe you should look into another line of work."

"What. Like a police officer?"

"No." She sips her coffee, thinking. "I don't know, something with writing … like a job in advertising?"

"Bossy Brooke," Vera answers with a wink. "Always looking at my life through one of these." She reaches into her tweed jacket pocket and pulls out a mini-magnifying glass.

"Dad's been at it again, I see." Brooke pulls her own magnifier from her denim jacket pocket. "You always know when snow season is around the corner."

"Yup. New magnifying glasses for all." Vera slips hers back in her pocket. "Dad's been up to other stuff, too. He's checking at the station to see if they can use me as a reporter there."

"Really, Vera? Dad's going to line up a job for you now? And you're freelancing with fluff articles? Plus fixing up an old home to boot and maybe renting a barn? Do you hear how chaotic your life's become? There's no pattern to your days, no routine. No plan."

Vera sighs, then moves on to the scarecrow horses in front of the small stable a block away. Beyond the stable, Addison's covered bridge is framed with tall maples brilliant in red-and-gold foliage. The bridge is a pretty time machine; when you pass through it, it brings you into historic Olde Addison and its vintage antique homes, wide tree-lined streets and the silver expanse of the cove, the destination of so many long-ago ship captains returning from trade at sea.

But here in the present, Brooke's right, in a way. Vera's hand slips into her pocket for her ballot and feels the magnifier there. Her father never wants them to miss a chance to see a snowflake up close, including a perfect icy specimen that might fall gently from the sky onto their sleeves.

The thing is, if she's learned anything about snowflakes from her father, it's this: Their pretty patterned shapes of star-like crystals and hexagonal plates might seem random, but they're not. Specific scientific conditions that seem arbitrary—from physics to math to chemistry—combine to determine each one's precise formation. There's nothing random about the shape of a snowflake that tumbles from the clouds. And that's the beauty of looking at them up close. Each delicate flake tells a unique and complex story about its form and pattern.

That's all she wants, really. Some of that distinct, snowflake structure in her own life. A structure that brings what looks like random choices and arbitrary wishes together in a very certain pattern.

Derek sweeps up sanding powder and dumps it in Vera's trash can, brushing the dust off his denim shirt, too. He hears her car door slam and figures he's got a minute or two to throw his tools together and be on his way. As he's carrying the toolbox to the kitchen, Vera breezes in through the side door in a rush of cold air and packages, and hurries to drop them on the round pedestal kitchen table.

"Hey, Derek. Finished?"

"I am, you're all set to paint the wall now." He sets

down the toolbox and resettles his cap backward on his head.

"Terrific! Let me pay you before you leave then." She pulls a checkbook from her shoulder bag and quickly writes out a check, which he folds in half and tucks in his shirt pocket. "I really appreciate it," she says while slipping out of a tweed jacket and hanging it on the back of one of the white-painted mismatched chairs: a Windsor, a couple ladder-backs, a cottage and a café style.

"No problem, Vera. Any time."

"Seriously?" she asks, her hazel eyes squinting at him.

"What?"

"Are you serious about *any* time? Because I actually have a few more things I need fixed, I just never personally knew someone who could do the work."

He shrugs. "What kind of work are we talking about?"

"Come on," she says, turning back and walking through the double-wide doorway into the dining room and then through to the living room. A striped sofa sits beneath two paned windows on the side wall, facing a large brick fireplace. "They're little things, really. But a lot of little things. Like this." She stops at the bottom of the staircase and shakes the large acorn finial on the banister leading upstairs along a soft cream wall.

"That's it?"

"To begin with. I have a list. Bad windows that stick. A warped door that closes only sometimes. The banister." She nods at the acorn. "Loose floorboards. A widow's walk that needs painting."

"Well I can do the work, if you don't mind sporadic. We're getting busy at the store with winter and the holidays coming up."

She follows him back into the kitchen and sits at the

round table, shifting over a bag she'd carried in. "This is good, actually. I'm kind of low on funds at the moment, so a little at a time works."

He picks up his toolbox and turns back to look at her for a second.

"What?" she asks, smiling a little uncomfortably.

"Home-cooked dinners work for payment, too."

"Ha." She stands quickly, scraping her chair across the floor, then reaches for a glass in the cupboard and pours herself a drink of water. "You might not say that if you tasted my cooking." She tucks her long layered hair behind an ear, looks around and rushes for the bag on the kitchen table. "And anyway, my sister's the chef, not me. Here. Why don't you take these?"

He reaches for the bag she holds out.

"They're coffee cakes. A ton of them. She just gave them to me at that scarecrow thing going on, and I'll never eat them all. Really. You have them. Those should hold you over until your next repair job."

"Your sister." He sets the bag inside his toolbox. "That'd be Brooke?"

She nods. "You know her?"

"Her husband does our books at the store. I was at the wedding."

"Wait …"

And she's doing it again, squinting those pretty hazel eyes at him when his cell phone rings. He glances at it, then up at her. "I can't miss this call," he says, picking up his toolbox filled with coffee cakes. "I'll see you around, Vera," he calls over his shoulder while walking out the side door.

Never bury the lead. The tenets of Journalism 101 always seem the most important, even after all this time. Vera sits in the downstairs office she set up, a brass lamp casting a yellow glow on papers scattered around her computer, her feet tucked into fuzzy snowflake slippers beneath the desk. Okay, so she didn't *really* have an assignment from the *Addison Weekly*. But maybe if she writes a snappy piece on the scarecrows, they'll use it. And pay her. So she's kind of making her own assignment. Sometimes you have to take the initiative.

With fingers hovering over the keyboard, she considers the lead she can't bury and finds herself instead typing headlines that *could* happen if things don't change soon, headlines she can't get out of her head: Local Resident Loses Life Savings to Fixer-Upper. Or Addison Native Penniless, Homeless and Jobless.

"No way. I can't go there. Not yet," she says as she opens a new document, sits up straighter and considers her real lead for the intensely competitive tradition pitting business against business, neighbor against neighbor, in a friendly contest for the town scarecrow trophy. The winner gets to display the gold trophy prominently, and with bragging rights, until the following autumn when it's passed along to the next Scarecrow of the Year.

"Focus," she whispers, opening her eyes wide and looking at the blank screen. She thinks long about the title, takes a quick breath and types as if her life depends on it. Which, she figures, it actually does. And so she better get serious.

Scarecrows Compete for Top Cawing
– By Vera Sterling

four

IT BEGINS WITH THE PUMPKINS. Little by little, they start showing up: on doorsteps, at lampposts, with mums, around cornstalks. Then come the apples and hay bales and gourds spilling from the farm stands. In Addison, Vera thinks the harvest scene is a sublimely perfect piece of art, a living watercolor painting of rich color applied with brush strokes of sunshine, dabbles of rainfall, and the patience of summer heat.

And the town Apple Festival puts it all on display. She walks through the cove park, passing the tall Ferris wheel reflected in the cove's calm October waters. Spinning wheels of chance, whirling carnival rides, craft tents, and people everywhere celebrate the annual harvest. She stops at Brooke's baked-goods booth to help her sister keep up with the sales.

"I'm trying to line these up in order," Brooke says, sliding her wrapped pastries around on shelves.

"Wait," Vera says. "Do you have a marker and paper? If you label them it'll help your customers know what they all are."

Brooke opens her tapestry tote, the one covered in stitched apples of every variety, and pulls out orange cardboard squares. "I was going to label them earlier, but it got too busy."

Vera takes the squares from her and begins writing: *Mini Apple Pies*, *Apple Crumb Coffee Cakes*. "Derek's been over to the house, fixing up some of its issues. The wall, the banister, you know, that kind of stuff." She takes another label and writes *Apple Tarts* across it.

"Derek?"

"From the hardware store," Vera says, lining up the *Tart* sign precisely with Brooke's freshly baked tarts.

"Oh, *that* Derek. It's good you're getting some work done. Does he ever talk about his daughter?" Brooke counts out change for a woman who bought one of her apple pies. "Thank you," she says while handing her the coins.

"Daughter?" Vera looks over at her. "I didn't know he had kids. Or that he was married."

"Divorced." Brooke realigns the pies to fill the vacant space from the one she'd just sold. "And he doesn't have kids now. His little girl Abby died, oh, must be five years ago. Drowned, right here actually. At the cove."

"No way!"

Brooke nods with a glance at Vera. "It was a terrible accident. She went through thin ice one afternoon, walking home from school with her friends. I guess they wanted to see if they could skate that weekend and tested it and, well, a couple kids went through. They couldn't save Abby."

"I had no idea. Oh my God, that's awful." When Brooke is busy selling a half-dozen mini apple muffins to a family waiting with full appetites, Vera takes another orange label and writes *Caramel Apple Cookies* across it. But her mind is still grappling with Derek's loss.

"Don't forget napkins!" Brooke reminds the family leaving with their pastries, which they've already begun eating. The father turns back and takes a handful from her. "It's Derek who runs the Deck the Boats Festival every December. That's when his daughter died, right around Christmas. He gets the decorated boats out there on the cove to commemorate her every year."

"Hey, guys," a woman calls out as she approaches the booth. "How've you been?"

"Hold that thought," Vera quickly tells her sister, wanting to know more about this Derek and getting a little impatient with the interruptions. She looks out at a woman with wavy blonde hair, wearing a long lace skirt, fitted sweater and suede ankle boots, carrying a large leather portfolio beneath her arm.

"Lauren?" Brooke asks.

"Brooke. And Vera! How nice to see you both," Lauren says, leaning over the booth counter to give them a hug.

"Lauren? Lauren Bradford?" Vera pulls back and eyes her closely. "Aren't you a blast from the past, bringing me right back to our old beach days."

"And I've spent a lot of time at Stony Point this summer. Have you been down lately?"

"Not this year. I just moved back to town, actually." Vera hitches her head toward her moss-green Dutch sitting on the edge of the cove property, the white railing of the widow's walk facing the water. "I've been busy with the move. Into that house right there."

"No kidding." Lauren studies the imposing home. "Holy cow, it's gorgeous. And on the water, no less." She looks back at Vera. "Still writing, too?"

"You bet. Locally now."

Lauren reaches into her portfolio and pulls out a painting of a historical home done on an antique plank of barnwood. "Any chance you could give my work a local plug? I've got a small display set up over beside the carousel if you'd like to see more."

Brooke takes the painting from her. "Wow, this is beautiful."

Vera looks too, and recognizes the brick-red saltbox colonial from a couple blocks down Main Street. "You'll do well selling these here. A little bit of Addison history."

"The antique shop in town is hosting a formal exhibit next month," Lauren tells them. "I've got lots of landmarks and homes I'm working on."

"The antique shop? Circa 1765?" Vera asks. "Sara Beth's hosting your work?"

"Yes! Do you know her?"

"We grew up practically next door to each other," Vera explains. "Hey," she continues, eyeing Lauren.

"Oh, no." Lauren shakes her head with a smile. "I remember that scheming look of yours from the old summer days hanging out on the boardwalk with nothing much to do. What do you have cooking behind those eyes?"

"It's good," Vera assures her, leaning over and squeezing her arm. "It's all good, no getting in trouble this time, I promise," she adds with a wink. And before Lauren returns to her art display, Vera secures her phone number and an interview date for an in-depth profile on her craft of barnwood art. The local historic angle will be perfect for the *Addison Weekly*.

❧

Today probably wasn't the best day to get started on more repairs of Vera's house. But with everyone in town at the Apple Festival, Derek figured the store would be quiet and he could cut out early to chip away at her list. He didn't count on the traffic, though, and people, and carousel songs and laughter coming in through the drafty windows of her neglected place, muffling the sound of her creaking wood floors and temperamental radiators. Happiness is not what he cares to associate with the cove.

After he tightens the new hinges on the pantry door, he hears Vera come in.

"Hey, Derek," she says, setting her handbag down on the kitchen table. "What great weather they've got for the fair. Just the right nip in the air today."

He doesn't say anything as he runs his hand over the door edge where it still sticks. But he does throw a glance her way, seeing her walk to the counter wearing skinny jeans tucked into slouchy boots. When she reaches for coffee grounds from a burgundy-painted cabinet, a rose-gold watch is visible beneath her sleeve.

"Have you been yet?" she asks over her shoulder while filling the coffee decanter with water.

He looks at her again while her back is to him, her long sandy-blonde hair fanned out across her black blazer, then pulls out a staple his hand catches on the door edge.

"To the fair?" she continues while pouring the water into the pot. "It's mobbed there today."

He rubs his knuckle against his jawline. "I don't really do fairs."

"Really? Aw, you should! My sister's serving up her famous apple-crumb coffee cake, Derek. You'd like it."

He shrugs, just slightly, and turns back to the pantry door edge he's preparing to plane. And when he cuffs his flannel shirtsleeves, that's when he notices how quiet the room's gotten. So he knows. He knows that *she* knows. Someone at the fair told her about Abby; nothing else would silence her like that except for the uncomfortable realization of why he doesn't want to be at a fair at the cove.

"Vera," he says. "Maybe today's not the best day for me to be working here."

She nods slightly, that's it, nothing else.

So he unplugs the planer and sets it aside, then swings the door to be sure the new hinges are working okay. "You'll be all set for now with your pantry. The door works, but it still sticks. I'll finish it up next trip."

"Sure. No problem."

"Do you mind if I leave some of these tools here so I'm not hauling them back and forth? I can store them in the barn, if that's all right, and come back another time."

"Oh geez, the barn."

"What's the matter with the barn?"

"Well the barn's okay, it's what's in it that worries me. I've been meaning to clean it up so I can rent it out for storage. But I think I've got a rodent issue."

"Rodents?"

"Maybe a raccoon? When I've tried sweeping the place out, I've seen it scoot past me, from the corner of my eye. Then I get spooked and run out."

"Okay, a raccoon. I've got a flashlight in my toolbox. I'll take a look around and leave my tools there for now." He grabs his corduroy quilted vest off the table and picks up the toolbox to leave.

"Wait," Vera says. "It's all locked up. Let me grab a flashlight and I'll go with you."

They walk outside, and the noise and festivities from

the Apple Festival still linger. The barn sits behind her house, off to the side and nestled in a gently sloping hill. It rises tall in the late-afternoon sunlight, its unpainted timber walls aged to varying shades of brown and silver. Derek won't even glance over at the cove park. He doesn't want to have a passing thought of what could have been. Doesn't want to see a girl holding a balloon, or eating a candied apple, or getting off a spinning ride and laughing in the sunshine, a girl with long brown hair who might be about Abby's age now. He doesn't want to picture his daughter, had she lived.

Vera stops at what used to be the Christmas Barn's main entrance. The red-painted door with paned windows looks as distressed as it sounds, creaking as she pulls the wrought-iron door pull and goes in ahead of him. The space is dim and musty, and he feels the damp from it being closed up and unused for so long. He checks his watch, then shines the flashlight beam into dark corners, along the planked walls, beneath empty wooden shelves and up along the ceiling's hand-hewn barn beams. The empty space definitely could shelter an animal of some sort.

"It was kind of big, and gray and brown. The last time I saw it," Vera is saying from off in a corner, "it ran in this direction."

Derek scans the floor and loft above while slowly backing toward the rear of the barn. Muffled sounds from the Apple Festival make their way into the shadowy space and it all feels unreal, like it's some disturbing dream, the commotion and sense of movement outside, and the dusky lighting and dust swirling in the cool, damp barn. It becomes a cyclone, spinning together in an incoherent sensation that he feels from time to time, in the right situation. One that breaks his heart when he fears that Abby felt a similar sensation of movement and blur and dusk and voices beneath the water's surface.

He jumps when Vera bumps right into his back, and she jumps at the same time, her hand to her heart, her flashlight clattering to the floor. "Oh gosh, I'm sorry. I didn't see you there."

She quickly steps back and goes to pick up the light the instant he does, their hands touching as they reach for it together. "No harm done," he says, handing it to her.

"Now you know what I mean when I get spooked in here thinking of those beady raccoon eyes watching me from some dark corner." Her flashlight beam sweeps once across the room before she snaps it off. "I don't know. I'm sure whatever it is, it's hiding now."

Derek gives a last look around, promising to bring traps from the store next time. Heading outside to his pickup truck, if nothing else, he's glad for their own commotion over raccoons and dropped flashlights and bumping into each other and the momentary distraction of Vera.

five

My LATEST NEIGHBORHOOD POLL INDICATES heavy nut-burying activity, more so in the eastern side of town. There's still time to let me know what squirrel trends you're seeing because for all the weather technology we have, sometimes Mother Nature knows best. And so far, the squirrels are busy preparing for very cold months ahead."

Vera knows before she even turns around that her father is giving his annual Addison Almanac winter weather predictions. It's the down-home, folksy stuff like this that makes him Addison's favorite meteorologist celebrity. She tightens the sash on her blue fluffy bathrobe and pours a mug of hot coffee, all the while listening to his winter trivia on the countertop television set.

"Just how cold will the winter be? By golly, pet your pooch to check. My dog Captain's coat of fur has gotten so thick, it rivals a beaver's, correlating nicely with recent squirrel behaviors. And that means only one thing: Lots of cold, cold weather is on the way."

Vera glances at her home's single-pane windows and

hopes her father is wrong. Cold air will seep right through the glass and make her chilly all winter. But he's never wrong. And if he's busted out his snowflake tie, then she knows they're all fated to a winter of white, too. She takes a peek at the TV screen, letting out an exasperated breath at the sight of the wide navy tie dotted with white snowflakes beneath his suit jacket.

"Now here's a secret I've kept since summer," he continues. "For every foggy morning in August—"

"There'll be a snowy day in winter," Vera finishes, smiling as she does. Every snow axiom, adage, proverb and saying is part of her stock vocabulary.

"So we're in for a doozy. Gas up the snow blowers, and if the woolly bear caterpillars are any indication, stock up on mittens and hats while you're at it. Take a look at these viewer photos sent in." Images of the brown-and-gold caterpillars fill her screen, some sitting on a leaf, some on extended hands. "Those narrow brown bands of fuzz in the middle mean a cold winter ahead. Which will be ideal for snow-watching. And by the way, you can snow-gaze all you like, but you won't find two identical snowflakes, folks."

Images of past snowstorms fill the screen while her father continues with his snow lore. "And here's why: The exact shape of each and every flake is defined by its chance twists and turns and spins as it free-falls from the clouds to the earth. It starts as one shape, but changes dramatically during its fall because every movement it makes affects its symmetrical shape. And no one flake will duplicate another because no two snowflakes take the same, precise path."

Well, now. Enough talk of predictions. Because Vera has her own gauges for predictions, and they're not looking pretty. One gauge would be a nearly empty checkbook. It forecasts a rough winter ahead just as well as the nut-burying squirrels do. If only she could stockpile her necessities to get through the coming months. There's only one way to do that—with a job. So she shuts off the television, sets her coffee mug in the sink and puts on her favorite forest-green sheath along with gold stud earrings and a big gold watch. Then, pressing a hand to her paned living room window to feel the temperature of the air leaking in, she decides on her brown leather bomber over it all and sets out for the *Addison Weekly*.

"Anything. I'll take anything," she tells the editor there as he's skimming her completed profile of Lauren Bradford and the barnwood art exhibit planned at Circa 1765.

He looks up at her pacing in front of his desk. "I like this."

"You do?" she asks, stopping still.

"Sure, it's got a nice local flavor. And who knows, some of our readers might commission the artist to paint their homes, too. I might like one for a Christmas gift for my wife, actually. So, yes. I'll use this in a few weeks."

Every bit of breath that Vera hadn't realized she'd been holding expels in a quick tearful sigh. "Seriously?"

"Definitely."

"For pay?"

He laughs. "Of course. Listen, you've proven yourself with the scarecrow piece, and now this. So I can put you on the payroll, part-time, but it'll be *regular* part-time work."

"I'll take it. Thank you, thank you, thank you."

"Stop at Bonnie's desk on the way out. She'll have forms you'll need to complete. It's a formality. Since you'll be on the payroll now."

"Wonderful." Vera extends her hand to shake his.

"Glad to have you on board, Vera. And thrilled to have one of Boston's top journalists working here. Actually, I've got an exclusive that might be right up your alley."

"Really?" Visions of in-depth reporting fill her thoughts. She's been away from the big time for so long, but it all comes easily back with the suggestion of it. Research, and tracking down leads, and verifying facts. "I've got references from Boston, if you need any."

"No, that won't be necessary, Miss Sterling. Although this one's under a tight deadline, so I hope you can handle the pressure. I'm giving you the Holly Trolley exclusive."

"The what?"

"Holly Trolley exclusive. It's mid-October already, so it'll be starting its holiday rounds soon. I need a driver interview, some history, maybe a firsthand look at a ride around town. What do you think?" he asks with a twinkle in his eye. "You up to the challenge?"

"You're serious."

"Vera. It's the *Addison Weekly*. It's what we do."

She looks long at him, squinting. "Well, I've never met a challenge I couldn't rise to," she tells him. "I'll get right on it," she says while walking out of his office.

And so, like those squirrels burying acorns to get through the winter, she stockpiles one check from Lauren's profile and a future check from her latest coup, the trolley piece. Hopefully she can dig up a few more to sustain her over the coming months.

Outside, headed to her car, she glances up at the sky. The thing is, furry caterpillars and tree branches holding on to lingering leaves, none of it can predict beyond what she knows.

And what she knows is this: Sometimes it feels like she's free-falling through a storm of days, twisting and turning with job issues and a tired old house and a dwindling bank account, her life constantly changing shape, starting out one way and becoming something else along the way, just like one of her father's falling snowflakes.

The heavy, rusted latch feels like it hasn't been touched in years. Derek lifts it to unlock the side double doors from inside Vera's barn, opening them slowly to an expansive view of the cove. The far side of the water is lined with trees in full autumn color, reds and golds and yellows. Closer to the barn, tall cove grasses of pale green, topped with feathery silver seed, sway in the cold breeze, almost like a whisper. An old green wooden rowboat, its paint faded, its inside driftwood gray, is tied to a rickety old dock in the grasses. And he simply stands there and looks, then decides to finish the ham grinder he'd brought along in his toolbox, finish it right there in front of that serene view.

In five minutes, or fifteen, he can't be sure how many, he hears Vera's car pull in the driveway and so he folds up his napkin, closes up the double doors and goes back through the barn, exiting through the old Christmas Barn entrance facing her house. He waves to her after shutting the door behind him. "I set out those traps I told you about," he says over his shoulder, noticing her walk over wearing a green dress and bomber jacket. He wonders where she's coming from, dressed up like that. "They're live traps. Cages. So we can transport the animal elsewhere after we catch it."

"Thank goodness. Because I really need to get in there and start cleaning it out."

"No problem," he answers, turning up the collar on his cargo jacket and glancing at the gray sky.

"Did you see my dad on TV this morning, predicting the winter weather?"

"Never miss Leo Sterling's Addison Almanac. He may be right about the snow this year. I feel it in the air."

"It could snow every day and he'd be so happy." She pulls a magnifying glass from her jacket pocket. "He gives me these all the time, to look at snowflakes up close. Says you'll never get bored snow-watching, it's nature's artwork." A cold wind lifts off the cove water and Vera looks up to the widow's walk on her house roof. "I'm thinking I'll have a bird's-eye view of the snow this winter. You can see all the way out to the Connecticut River up there, which must've been the sea captain's intent when this house was built."

Derek looks up to her roof and zips his jacket against the wind.

"Come on inside and warm up. I'll put on coffee."

He glances out toward the sea captain's view of the water, then back at Vera who apparently isn't taking no for an answer, already headed quickly toward the side door into the house. "Sure, that sounds good," he calls after her.

"Be careful." She points down at one of the steps on the short flight of stairs. "That one's creaky."

He sets his boot on it and the soft wood gives beneath a little pressure. The edges are showing signs of rot, too. "You should add it to your list. I'd hate to see you hurt yourself if it gives out."

"Okay, but for now, I'll be stepping around it. At least

until my cash situation improves." She unlocks the door and they go into her kitchen. "Which, I'm happy to say, will be soon. I got a job today," she tells him with a little curtsy, then sets her purse on the counter.

"Well, congratulations," Derek says as he first looks back at the slamming screen door that needs a new spring, before slipping out of his jacket and draping it over the back of one of the distressed-white wooden chairs. A pendant light hangs over the round table from the painted beadboard ceiling, and a collection of red ceramic apples lines the countertop.

"It's not much, but it's a start. Writing for the *Addison Weekly*."

"Hey, not bad." He pulls out the chair to sit, watching as she puts coffee grounds into the coffeepot. "At least you're on familiar territory."

"I am. My first assignment is to write about the Holly Trolley. You know, before the Christmas season gets into full swing." She pulls two mugs from the burgundy cabinets and turns to him. "Speaking of which, I know it's not an easy time of year for you. Brooke told me about Abby, and I'm so sorry about your loss. It can't be easy."

"It's not, really. It's just something that's there. That we deal with."

After a quiet second, Vera asks what most people don't want to mention. "What happened, Derek?"

He hesitates, then turns up his hands. "You know kids. It got really cold for a few days that December and the water froze early on the cove. She was walking home from school with a couple friends, it was a Friday. And seeing all that ice, I don't know, I guess they got excited and wanted to test it. For skating." He waits while Vera fills his mug with hot coffee. "But it had just frozen and wasn't very thick. I got a call at work," he says while pouring cream into the cup. "To get to the cove right away." He folds up his shirt cuff and glances at his watch. "When I got there, they'd just found her."

"Oh, Derek." She sits across from him at the table and reaches over to give his arm a quick grasp.

"It wasn't good." He sips from his mug, shaking his head. "Another little girl went under too, but they'd gotten her out sooner and were able to save her. They just couldn't find Abby in time." He takes a long breath and slides his coffee away. "Her friends said she only took a few steps and was actually turning back when the ice gave out." He looks directly at Vera. "It happened, you know? It's just something that happened."

"You must miss her so much."

"I do." It's not necessary to say it doesn't get easier; it just gets different, over time. He feels, looking at her eyes, seeing her quiet, that she knows this somehow. "I have to tell you, Vera. I was looking out over the water from your barn earlier." He stands and lifts his coat off the chair back, talking as he slips it on. "I used to stay as far away from the cove as possible, but lately, I don't know. It's like I can sense her here. This property of yours, sitting on the edge of town, well, today I felt more peace than I have in a long time."

"I'm so glad for that," she tells him with a glance at the table. "You didn't finish your coffee?"

He checks his watch again, certain she's not aware that it's that time, Abby's time. "We're busy at the store. The wreaths and Christmas trees will be coming in soon and I've got to set out the stands. Then I'll be spending the weekend at my parents' garage getting the carriage and sleigh ready."

"Sleigh?"

"Depending on the weather. My uncle owns a small stable and a couple horses. So if it snows, we have a little red sleigh and give weekend holiday rides at the store." He talks while heading out, pulling his jacket up over his shoulders. "You know, a horse-drawn ride around the block. The folks love it."

Vera follows behind him to the door while he pulls his keys from his pocket. "Listen, Derek. I'm having a small housewarming party Saturday. It's my birthday, too, and my family will be here, a few friends. Brooke convinced me to have the get-together—gosh, she'll use any excuse to bake a cake. So anyway, you should come. It'll be fun."

"I'll be busy, Vera, so I'm not sure."

"Well, even after you clean up the carriage. It doesn't matter what time. We play a mean charades, a little Twister, have a glass of wine, a few laughs."

He reaches for the paned door and starts to open it. Vera still follows behind him; he can tell without turning, simply by the closeness of her voice. "I just thought, well, who doesn't like cake and coffee?"

Derek stops halfway out the door, checks his watch, then looks back at her. "We'll see."

six

<hr/>

T HE SKY SEEMS SOMEHOW BIGGER from up here, doesn't it?" Vera asks her father. Her mom and sister are down in the kitchen setting out the party plates, but Vera wanted to suggest something to her dad here on the widow's walk.

"It's a whole different perspective, opens up the view," her father answers as he circles the roof-walk, his hand on the white wooden railing. "I imagine the sea captain got a good handle on sailing conditions, seeing the river out there, watching the skies for change."

"Listen, Dad." She pulls her plaid scarf up around her head in the cold breeze and clutches it beneath her chin. "What do you think about doing a forecast from here? A segment when you're predicting snow? It's such a unique perspective, it would make for a great satellite forecast spot."

"Now that's not a bad idea, Vee."

They both look out at the silver water, which reflects the brilliant blue sky and churning puffy white clouds right back at them. "All that water," she adds quietly, "and it's so still, it's like a mirror. Those clouds are really vivid."

"What I'm thinking is that the cove water is a good source of vapor for snow clouds. I love the idea of filming a segment up here. It could be very dramatic."

Vera paces, holding her scarf tied close, her shoulders hunched against the cold. "Okay, we'll plan on it, then. But let's get inside before I freeze!"

"Hey," her father says, stopping her as he runs his hand along the railing. "Check this out. You've got twinkly lights."

Vera sees that the white railing and vertical spindles—okay, they need a coat of paint, too—are entwined with clear lights, the kind you'd put on a Christmas tree. "They must be left behind from the old days, Dad. Maybe when the Christmas Barn was in business?"

"I'll bet that's it. Is there a switch?"

"Inside, at the bottom of the stairs," Vera says. "Do you think they still work?"

Her father descends into the house and moments later, her entire widow's walk is illuminated with sparkling light. "Ooh! So pretty." She steps back laughing, looking at all the tiny twinkling lights. "Leave them on, Dad. It'll look festive all lit up for the party tonight."

"Right foot, yellow!"

"What?" Brooke asks. "Right foot? I can't untangle it—wait."

"Right hand, blue!" Vera shouts, watching Brooke nearly fall over onto Brett, her long brown hair sweeping across the dotted mat. The guys had moved the sofa out of the way earlier so they'd have room to play. "Hey you two, keep it clean now. I mean, really, it's Twister."

Brett shifts his right hand beneath Brooke's leg to the nearest blue.

"Left hand, yellow!"

"Yellow?" Sara Beth asks. Her husband, Tom, puts his hand on the same yellow spot his foot is on. "Hey, is that legal?"

Brooke glances over, then loses her balance and falls flat on her back, throwing out her arms in exasperation.

"You're out," Brett tells her as she skulks off.

"I'm so done with this silly game," she answers from the striped couch where she pulls ankle boots on over her stockinged feet. "Twisting me up like that," she says.

"What's wrong with twisting up a little?" Brett asks her, and Vera just catches the wink he throws her way.

Vera gives the spinner another whirl and Brooke takes it from her. "Mom wants you in the kitchen. I think she needs help wrapping the leftover pizza."

"I'm on it."

Her sister glares over at Brett then. "Huh. Let's see you try this one. Right hand, red."

In the kitchen, her mother is writing down a phone number. "What's up, Mom? Need help cleaning?"

"No thanks, it's all finished. I'm ready to put out the cake and coffee." Vera's collection of vintage coffee cups and saucers are set on a tray, looking like fine, antique artwork. Most are hand-painted florals, some edged in gold, some with ornate looping handles, a couple black-and-white striped. "But here, take this number first." Her mother rips a page from the pad on the kitchen countertop. "It's the Marches' phone number. They're really interested in renting out your barn. As soon as possible."

"Seriously?"

"Oh yes. They lost their carriage house in a fire last year, remember? So they need storage space until they rebuild. But that won't be until the spring, maybe even next summer."

"Wow, this comes at such a good time."

"Can I see it? I told Lillian I'd take a look to see how much space there is."

"Sure." Vera presses the back of her hand to the kitchen window near the doorway.

"What are you doing?" her mother asks.

"This?" Vera returns her hand to the glass. "Come here, I'll show you." Her mother steps close and Vera takes her fingers and holds them to the window. "Feel that?"

"Yes! It's very drafty. I feel cold air."

"Right." Vera lifts her scarf and bomber jacket from a Windsor chair back. "That's how I check which coat to wear."

"Are you serious?" her mother asks, feeling the window temperature again.

Vera shrugs. "Come on, I'll show you the barn now, before we serve dessert. A couple lights work in there, so you'll get a good idea anyway. How soon do they want it?"

"Right away, as soon as you get it cleaned up." Her mother slips into her jacket, pulling gloves from the pockets as she goes. "According to your window, I need to wear these."

Vera flips on the outside light at the side door and heads quickly down the steps, excited to show her mother the space. Dried leaves crunch beneath her feet in the chill air. "I think it'll be perfect for them," she is saying when she hears a loud crack of wood and her mother calling out in surprise. "Mom?"

"Oh Vera, what the hell? I'm stuck, for God's sake."

Vera hurries back to her mother kneeling awkwardly on the steps. "What happened?"

"My foot went right through the wood! Shoot, I think I broke it."

"Can you move it?" Vera takes her mother's hand to help her straighten up.

"I don't think so. Ow, ow, ow! It hurts like the dickens. Maybe you should get Dad."

"Really?"

Her mother nods in the dark. "He can help me up. I'm not sure I can walk on it."

"Oh God, hang on then," Vera tells her as she rushes inside for her father.

And all she thinks as her father helps her mother to her feet and hobbles with her to the car, telling her, "It's all right, Judy, we'll get you checked out," and as Brooke and Brett send the other party guests on their way into the frosty night with wrapped-up birthday cake slices, and as she rushes through the rooms turning off lights and picking up dirty dishes and half-empty drink glasses and dropping them into the soapy dishwater to soak, and as Brett drives her and Brooke along the dark roads to the hospital emergency room to check on their mother, and as they stop at the railroad crossing while a freight train passes by, and as Brooke tells her from the front seat that she should flip that dumpy house and be done with it ... well, she thinks this one thought: Why oh why didn't she listen to Derek and have him repair that gosh-darn step?

The pickup truck's tires crunch over leaves and twigs from the big maple tree when he turns into Vera's driveway. Derek drags his hand back through his still-damp hair. After waxing the sleigh and tuning up the carriage all afternoon, he'd taken a quick shower before leaving for Vera's party.

But something's off. The house is dark, no cars are in the driveway, and only a couple dim lights shine in the windows. Unless he's somehow mistaken, the house is empty: the curtains are still, no television light flickers in any window, the doors are all closed up, the stoop light off. There's not a sign of life. His eyes rise to the rooftop. Except for that widow's walk, with the thin railing and every white spindle twinkling in hundreds of little white lights. So is someone up there?

He shuts off the engine and glances at the large, flat box wrapped in bright gift paper on the passenger seat beside him. Then his eyes return to the big old Dutch colonial, looking for any sign of movement, of someone at home, of Vera. A cornstalk is tied to her lamppost with two pumpkins set at its base, but even the lamppost is off. Finally he gets out and goes to her front door, stepping around a potted mum and ringing the bell only once before heading around to the side door, walking between the shadowed barn and the house. The wind from earlier in the day had stopped with the sun setting, and so it's calm and cold outside. He's aware of the dark cove off in the distance even though he can't see it in the black night. But just knowing it's there, unseen, draws him closer.

Sometimes he takes a ride at night, parking near the water to say the few words of comfort he never had a chance to say. Not often, but three or four times since Abby died he's been drawn to do so. He looks over at

Vera's apparently empty house, annoyed at her invitation that fell through, and instead of trying the side door, takes a few steps toward the dark cove then, his boots stepping on dried fallen leaves. Getting closer, he can hear the soft, gentle lapping of water shifting along the shore and he stops.

"It's okay," he whispers after a long moment, then waits, still listening to the water. Knowing his daughter's last moments were spent beneath it makes it hard for him to hate it. He used to, but he's gradually come to feel that the water gives life to some part of her, to her spirit. "You didn't know the ice would break. I'm not mad at you, so don't be crying now." He glances over his shoulder at the twinkling lights on Vera's widow's walk rising to the night sky, then smiles in the dark. "It's pretty, isn't it?" he whispers, flipping up his jacket collar against the cold air. "Little stars, Abby, twinkling happy, just for you."

seven

WHATEVER HAPPENED, IT'S BAD. VERA can see that clearly beneath the harsh glare of the hospital lighting. The man sits leaning forward in the waiting room, his elbows on his knees, his face cupped in his hands. He is completely in the moment, completely distraught at whatever diagnosis an emergency room physician delivered to him about someone he loves.

She looks over at Brooke, tipping her head toward the distraught man and feeling just as worried, ready to hurry to the nurse station until she spots her father returning. "All's good," he tells them quietly as he scoots a chair close to her, Brooke and Brett.

"She's okay?" Brett asks, tucking away the cell phone he'd been checking for football scores.

Her father nods. "A very serious sprain, but nothing's broken." He looks back toward the busy examining rooms. "The doctor's almost done, so she'll be out in a sec. It'll be a day or two before the swelling goes down, but she'll be fine."

Vera can't help but glance over at the other fellow in

the waiting room, the one who hasn't moved at all, his face and worry still covered in his cupped hands. It's one of those moments when twists of fate separate some from others and it always breaks your heart, regardless.

"Rest, ice and elevation," she hears then, and turns to see her mother being pushed out in a wheelchair by a tall, fair doctor with blue eyes she remembers and a vaguely familiar face. He gives orders while walking along in pale green scrubs.

"Greg?" Vera stands quickly. "You're Mom's doctor?"

"How are you, Vera?" he asks back, nodding. "Judy's been a good patient. No worries."

"You work *here*?"

"When I'm not dancing at weddings with beautiful women." He pauses, then looks from her mother, then back to her. "Sometimes I cover a shift in the ER."

"And he's the best orthopedic surgeon the hospital could have, I'll tell you that," Vera's mother says from the wheelchair. "I'm feeling better already."

"Well then. Orthopedic surgeon, you say?" Vera repeats as she lifts her bomber jacket from the chair back. "I guess you weren't kidding at the wedding."

"What do you mean?" he asks, smiling lightly at her.

"When you said you fix things all day?"

He shrugs. "You've got a good memory."

"Mom?" Brooke stands and pulls her car keys from her purse. "You're all set to go home?"

"She is," Greg tells them. "But stay off that foot for a few days, Judy, and definitely keep it iced and elevated."

"Doctor's orders, I know," her mother assures him.

"I hear a celebration was going on when all this happened," Greg says to Vera.

"I told him it was your birthday," her mother lets on

as her father helps her out of the wheelchair. Brett and her father each take an arm and begin slowly walking her toward the exit.

"And I'd like to toast your day, Vera," Greg suggests. "I'm just finishing up here for the night and would love to take you out for a birthday drink."

"That's awfully nice of you," Vera begins, ready to decline until she sees it all: Brooke not missing a trick and raising a discreet eyebrow, Brett checking his watch to gauge how much more of the football game he's missing, her father taking a step toward the door anxious to get home while clasping her mother's arm, and her mother smiling at Vera. After all, it *is* Vera's birthday.

"Mom? You'll be okay without me?"

"Don't worry, we've got her covered," Brooke insists. "We'll get her settled at home. You go, have a good time."

"Okay, then." She turns to Greg. Gregory Davis, orthopedic surgeon, apparently. "I'll wait here for you?" And like that, the night shifts. Her family leaves, the doctor promises he'll shed the scrubs and be back shortly, and the waiting room gentleman leaning into his hands is rushing down the hallway beside a nurse now, his demeanor changed with whatever she says, his step quick and hopeful.

After being in the harsh lighting of the hospital emergency room, this is nice. Walking into Cedar Ridge Tavern, Vera sees the amber pendant lights hanging over the dark walnut bar. *Breathe,* she thinks. *Mom's fine.* Even though it was Vera's fault for not fixing that darn step. She jumps when Greg takes her elbow to lead her through the room.

"Hey, you okay?" he asks.

"It's really been a crazy night, I guess I'm a little on edge. Like, we started out playing Twister and ended up in the hospital, you know what I mean?"

"It happens," he assures her. "I'm glad your mom is okay."

"Me, too." They approach the long bar decorated with large illuminated twig pumpkins set on either end, and a berry-and-autumn-leaf garland strung on the wall behind it, over the mirror. Only a few people sit at the bar; the real crowd is relaxing at the tables on the other side of a half-wall, closer to the roaring fire burning in the stone fireplace.

But something catches her attention and Vera's gaze shifts from the fireplace back to the mirror behind the bar. And when she notices Derek's reflection over on the side at the far end, she suddenly remembers her invitation. "Oh shit," she whispers, tugging on Greg's arm to slow him. "Greg, why don't we grab a table? It'll be nice by the fire."

"Maybe later," he answers, still walking. "It's more festive over here. You know, for your celebration." He leans on the curved end of the bar right beneath one of the amber lights, takes a look at the five or six people sitting at it and signals the bartender. "Drinks for everyone here at the bar," he tells him, lifting his foot onto the brass foot rail. "Celebrating is in order for a special birthday," he announces, backing up a step and motioning to Vera behind him.

Vera shifts her stance, pushing her hair behind an ear and giving a small wave to the people sitting at the bar turning to look at her. Some wish her *happy birthday*, some *the very best*, and one, the one at the far end, gives her a slow look if ever there was one. Oh, she feels every bit of its journey from the top of her leather bomber jacket right down her cuffed jeans to the silver-metallic oxfords she chose for her party. Yup, the party she *wasn't* at when she just knows he arrived. She closes her eyes for a long second, one long enough to take that real deep breath that says she has a lot of explaining to do.

Derek lifts his glass in her direction, his gaze shifting from hers to the doctor and back to her.

"Greg," she says quietly, her hand on his arm. "Excuse me for one second, there's someone here I want to say hello to."

"Sure, go ahead," Greg answers while scanning the patrons for the familiar face.

She gives him a quick smile and hushed thanks and works her way around the people at the bar turning to toast her big day, finally reaching Derek.

"Happy birthday, Vera," Derek says when she sits on the barstool beside him. He turns to face her, leaning an arm on the bar, his eyes never leaving hers.

"Derek." She looks at him with a regretful breath. "Listen, I don't suppose you stopped by my place."

"I did."

"I'm so sorry. We were there, honest. Everyone was there, we had food, some good times going on. I feel terrible that I missed you. It's just that my mother, well, you know that step you told me to fix?"

He just looks at her silently.

So she laughs a small laugh, rolling her eyes as she does. "Wouldn't you know it? Someone went right through it. My mom did and we had to rush her to the hospital. Her foot was hurt pretty bad. And it all happened so fast. I mean, I wrapped up the cake to-go and sent everyone on their way and closed up the house quick so we could get there, and the time ... I guess it got away from me."

"Sure, Vera." Derek stands and lifts a brown leather jacket with a sherpa-lined collar from the stool back.

What she sees, from the rust-colored Henley sweater over a button-down shirt and the jacket and the dark denim jeans, well, she sees he'd headed out to a party tonight. Hers.

"You're leaving?" she asks.

He only nods, slipping into the jacket easily and shifting it on his shoulders.

"Derek, really. It completely slipped my mind, I got so distracted at the hospital."

"I'm sure you did," he says, pulling his keys from his pocket.

"No, really, and then I was so glad my mom was okay, and Greg, well, I know him from high school, and he was her doctor there and, well, he thought I shouldn't end my birthday—"

"I understand, Vera, you don't have to explain. It's no problem. You have a good night now and enjoy that birthday of yours." He pulls out his wallet and leaves a tip on the bar before walking off toward the door, nodding at Greg as he passes him along the way.

And she watches Derek go, winding around crowded, candlelit tables, shaking hands and stopping to say a few words to someone he must know on the way, laughing then at whatever the man says before stepping around him and heading out. She keeps watching, swearing at herself for screwing up his plans, watching still as the door opens onto the cold October night before him, still watching as she stands and stamps her silver-oxford-clad foot on the floor when he flips up his collar against that dark, wavy hair and walks out, before she finally looks over at Greg, who'd been looking at her the whole time.

eight

Sɪɴᴄᴇ ᴛʜᴇ ɴɪɢʜᴛ ᴏꜰ ʜᴇʀ birthday, there's been a change in the air. All week, the cold fall mornings left Vera snuggled beneath a thick comforter covering her sleeping body. By Thursday, a chill wind rattles the windowpanes, and she hears the *click, click, click* of the tired furnace finally sending heat up through the pipes. So she pulls that soft comforter even closer beneath her chin, leaving her eyes closed and stealing a few more sweet minutes of sleep. It's that dreamy time when she just knows that outside, smoke rises from chimneys and gray clouds streak a blue sky and frost covers the pumpkins and—and that sound, that noise. She pulls the comforter up over her head to block out a banging. A banging that shouldn't be there in her bliss. Please, oh please don't let it be her furnace conking out. That's one expense that is not in the budget right now.

Then it stops, leaving only the clicking radiators filling with heat, tick-ticking as warmth fills the room. She breathes a sigh of relief, steals a look at her alarm clock from beneath the covers and is glad to see there's another thirty minutes of sleep waiting before she has to get up.

If it weren't for that gosh-darn banging starting up again.

"Fine," she says as she tosses back her flannel sheets and pulls on her bathrobe and fuzzy snowflake slippers. It comes again, in a rhythm of *four bangs, pause. Four bangs, pause.* Maybe she just has to adjust the thermostat, or give the furnace a little kick.

The noise grows louder as she goes downstairs, so loud that she realizes it's not coming from her basement furnace after all, but from outside. Again, *four bangs, pause,* but this time they come faster, and if it's at all possible, a little louder. And again, louder still. It must be someone working at the cove, maybe getting the small docks ready for winter. If that's the case, they can tone it down already—they're sounding rather mad the way that hammer is thudding. She decides to take a quick look to be sure that's all it is; there's a good view of the cove from near the barn. So she pulls her robe tight around her and rushes to the side door, hearing the noise even louder still, pushing open the door, looking out toward the cove and rushing down the stairs.

"Whoa, whoa there," Derek says as she nearly knocks him over. He's crouched on the middle step, his hands catching his balance on the step behind him.

"Derek?" She stops suddenly and looks at the lumber and tools and some take-out breakfast food off to the side.

"Good morning to you, too." He stands up, pulls off a glove, straightens it and puts it back on.

"What are you doing here? I mean, I thought someone was working at the cove with all that racket." And it's right then that she realizes how she looks and so moves backward, up a step, toward the privacy of the kitchen.

He pulls his black wool hat off and resettles it on his head, and she sees it, the way his darn brown eyes drop to her fluffy slippers and then back up to her tangled hair. "You said your mother hurt herself on this step," he explains.

"She did."

"And I didn't want anyone else getting hurt on my account."

"Your account?"

"I told you I'd fix it, so I'm fixing it, okay?"

She glances up at the brightening sky. "This early? It's not even seven."

He turns up his gloved hands. "Well, *I've* got things to do today. Sorry if I woke you."

She looks quickly down at her robe, then presses back a strand of mussed hair. "I just thought it was someone at the ..." She glances out toward the cove. "Well, it doesn't matter."

"If you don't mind then, I'll finish this up."

"Go ahead."

"You're in my way."

"Oh. Sorry."

He picks up a hammer and pulls a couple nails from his jacket pocket. "And I'm not sure about the rest of the stuff. You know, on that list of yours. Might not get to it till after the holidays."

"You mean, next year?"

"Vera, we're busy at the store. Christmas trees are coming, I've got to clear out space for the sleigh and carriage rides. I'll get to your repairs when I can."

"Okay, then. Fine." She turns and goes inside, briskly closing the paned door behind her and hearing Derek hammer more nails into the new step. With her back leaning on the door and her eyes momentarily closed, another four bangs break the morning's quiet, louder than ever if she's not mistaken. Slowly she turns and opens the door again to find him kneeling on the step holding a small level; a half-eaten bagel with cream cheese sits in its wrapping beside it. "Well, I'm making coffee. Would you like one, to go with that bagel?"

He stands and checks his watch. "No, I'm finishing up here. I'll check the traps in the barn and be on my way."

"You're sure? Because it's no trouble."

"Yup." He bends for his hammer then, tapping in the last few nails.

Inside, she ditches the robe and puts on a pair of faded jeans and a green cable-knit sweater. She adds a scarf around her neck while she's at it because even though the furnace wasn't the source of the noise and is working fine, the cold wind outside leaves a chill in her drafty house. As she pours coffee, there's a knock at her door and she opens it to see Derek there again.

"I caught your raccoon." He sets down a trap on the stoop.

"Oh my God," she says while jumping back with her hand to her heart. "Wait a minute, that's not a raccoon." She eyes the longhair gray tabby caught in the cage. A feline with tail fur that is black-ringed, like a raccoon's. "It's a cat!"

"That's right."

"What am I supposed to do with a cat?"

"Don't know." Derek turns and starts walking down the steps. "Keep it in the barn, I guess. It's a good mouser."

"Wait."

But he doesn't, raising his hand in a quick wave as he walks toward his pickup truck, gets in and backs down her long driveway.

"A mouser?" She steps outside and bends a little closer, watching the cat hunkered there with its paws folded beneath it, calm as could be, looking straight at her. "Swell," she says as she stands and goes inside for her coffee. Cupping the hot mug in her hands, she peers out the paned windows of her door down at the trapped cat still sitting on the stoop. "Just swell."

So Derek thought *he* was busy? Her days fly by with stripping floral dining room wallpaper and painting a living room accent wall, the floors covered with drop cloths and curled wallpaper scraps, her blonde hair pulled back beneath a bandana while Vera wields scrapers and paintbrushes until suddenly she can't believe it. It's the first week of November and the Holly Trolley deadline is looming. So until she gets her exclusive written, all home repairs are put on hold.

"You'll find so much information in our Archive Room," Bonnie says over her shoulder as she leads Vera down a long hallway in the *Addison Weekly* offices. "All the old issues and articles are only referenced on the computer, with the full papers actually stored along the walls. But recent years' issues are fully online and shelved, too. So a few clicks will get you all you need." She opens a door onto a bright and spacious room lined with too many shelves to count and long tables set up for research. "And be sure to replace any old papers in the right chronological spot."

Vera settles in behind one of the desktop computers and starts her search for previous Holly Trolley articles. In the last two years, several photographs were published, but no in-depth profiles. The images show that the vehicle is actually a small bus designed as a festive green-and-gold trolley. Swags of holly and berries, bells and white lights line the interior ceiling. And the interior slatted wooden benches look like exact replicas from another era. She'll have to research their origins, along with that of the twisted brass poles at the end of the rows of seats.

As she types various search words into the archive system, one particular headline catches her eye. She can't help but click on the link to read more and can't help the way her eyes skim the words quickly, looking for details, finding herself desperate to know.

A young girl died Friday afternoon after falling through the ice on Addison Cove, according to authorities … Seven-year-old Abigail Cooper pronounced dead at the scene … cause of death drowning … Members of the fire department's water rescue team worked valiantly to save Cooper and a second child after receiving a call for help from a passerby coming upon the incident. The children were testing the ice … thick enough for skating when it gave way beneath them … Cooper located after nearly twenty-five minutes beneath the frigid waters and no pulse could be detected … Though record cold temperatures, ice is still thin this early in the season … Authorities warn residents to exercise caution near any frozen body of water. The child's father, Derek Cooper, arrived on-scene … not available for comment.

The last line has her stop reading any further. Instead her eyes seek out the accompanying photographs of the emergency scene at the cove. The images are devastating, even now: ambulances, paramedics, fire trucks, men emerging from icy water wearing bright yellow insulated dive suits. And yes, there—Vera enlarges the image on the screen—there, off to the side. It looks like the fire marshal, Bob Hough, talking to Derek. She recognizes Derek right away from his stance, his brown hair, his eyes. He stands coatless beside the ambulance, hands shoved in his jean pockets, shoulders in a flannel shirt hunched against the biting cold, looking away from the fire marshal, not meeting his eye.

And she can see what the camera didn't capture because the moments that led to this sad image are clearly visible in his posture. What her mind sees is this: Derek running, desperately tearing out of his coat knowing they were only minutes too late, minutes, and he had to do something, anything at all for his little girl, something to help her. In his panic, his arm got tied up in a coat sleeve until he yanked it off for all he was worth. Because he had to, he had to do something just for her, to try to warm her small, wet body, to lay his warm coat over her and gently press it to her sides, his hand then running along her sodden hair and stroking her cold face, trying, trying to press life back into it until he finally just hugged her close, holding his face to hers. Yes, his coat must be laid over his child on the stretcher already lifted onto the ambulance.

It's all there in his stance in the one photograph, every sad bit of the last few urgent minutes that exhaustively defeated him.

nine

WITH THE DAYS GETTING SHORTER, Derek thinks he can at least get the boat washed before the sun sets, especially with his sister minding the store. This way it will be ready for waxing in the next few days, its first of several shines before the Deck the Boats Festival. Already the emails from his friends are arriving, reserving a spot in the procession for their vessels. He lifts a soapy sponge out of the bucket of water and walks around the trailered boat parked behind the hardware store. A swirl of dried leaves blows past and he glances up at the graying sky. "One section at a time," he says quietly as he works the sponge in a circular motion on a small part of the fiberglass boat's side. A stream of water dribbles down his sleeve and so he squeezes out the sponge, then continues. "We'll get it all cleaned up for you."

The customer service bell inside the store is wired to ring in the work area outside, too. He looks back over his shoulder when it chimes, drops the sponge into the soapy water and waits, taking his cap off and resettling it backward on his head again. After a few moments, he lifts the dripping sponge from the water bucket and continues. "What do you think, Abby, colored lights this year or white twinkly?" He'll have to pull the artificial tree off the storage shelf in the garage. "Maybe we'll put colored lights on it. First time," he adds, picturing the tree mounted on the boat's bow with the colored lights reflected on the dark water. "I think you'll like that."

The customer service bell rings again, a little longer this time, as someone waits for assistance inside. "Samantha!" he calls over his shoulder. His sister is supposed to be covering the store while he gets the boat cleaned. He moves toward the back of the boat, wiping the summer's grime off its surface. "It's an important step," he says under his breath, "so we don't rub the dirt right into the fiberglass when we wax it."

The bell gives two short chimes again. "Jesus, Sam, where the hell are you?" he calls out as he throws the sponge into the bucket and stands straight, his rubber-gloved hands on his hips. "You getting that?"

When no response comes back to him, no wisecrack call from his sister, he hurries down the driveway to the store, peeling off the wet gloves as he goes, walking inside to see Vera standing in faded jeans and a black fringed poncho at the checkout area. He sets his wet gloves down on the counter and turns up his hands. "What broke now?"

"What?" she asks, looking from him to the wet gloves and back to his face.

"Never mind." He shakes his head and when Samantha rushes into the store with a coffee to-go and box of doughnuts, he glares at her.

"What's the matter with you?" Samantha asks.

"What are you doing leaving the store empty?" Derek snaps back.

"I didn't. Tyler's here, somewhere."

"He's busy helping someone over near the paint," Vera interrupts. "He said I should ring the bell for assistance."

"We could get robbed," Derek warns Sam, "leaving the place practically empty like that."

She pulls a maple-frosted doughnut from the box and sets it on a napkin in front of him. "He's nicer after he eats," she calls to Vera while heading toward the back office.

Derek watches her go, then turns to Vera. "What do you need?"

"Oh." She adjusts her shoulder bag strap. "Well, I didn't know if you maybe carried pet bowls. And a cat bed. I guess that barn cat's sticking around, so I thought I could at least make him comfortable and give him some decent food. You know," she adds while raising an eyebrow, "besides mice."

Derek picks up the wet gloves and walks over to the far side of the store, stepping around the yellow lab sleeping in front of the electrical aisle. "Watch out for Zeus," he says over his shoulder. "He's my father's dog."

"The store mascot?" Vera asks from behind him.

"Something like that. He pretty much overlooks his kingdom, which *is* the store," Derek explains. He heads down an aisle of leashes and collars and catnip toys, with pet beds and bowls at the end. "There you go," he tells her while shoving the wet gloves in his cargo jacket pocket. Vera stands beside him looking at various silver bowls and ceramic dishes when he checks his watch. "You should be all set now. You and your cat."

"Derek," she says. "I was thinking." She takes a quick breath, then goes on. "Can I make it up to you?"

"Make what up to me?"

"The whole birthday thing, from a couple weeks ago. Because when you saw me and Greg at Cedar Ridge Tavern, well, it wasn't what you thought it was."

"And that would be?"

"I don't know. That I'm seeing him or something and stood you up. Because I didn't."

He rubs his knuckle along his jaw, looking at the cat bowls in front of them. "Yeah, sure," he finally says. "Okay."

"Really? Because I could so go for some pasta and Bella's is running a special. Are you free tonight? My treat?"

"The Italian place?" He pushes up his jacket sleeve, which is still damp from washing the boat, and checks his watch again. "I'll be done here around five. Pasta sounds good, Vera. On one condition, though."

"What's that?" she asks as her hand reaches out from beneath the poncho and picks up a cat bowl.

"It's on me, seriously."

"But I owe you one, for showing up at my nonexistent party." She drops the bowl into a small store basket hooked on her arm. "Which I'm still sorry about."

"Forget about that, okay? My treat, or no deal."

"Fine, then."

"Okay. I'll pick you up, Vera, after work. And stick with the shallow bowls."

"The what? Shallow?"

"For the cat." He walks away, headed toward that maple-frosted, his wet work boots squeaking on the wood floor. "They like the shallow bowls, it's easier for them to eat out of."

SNOWFLAKES AND COFFEE CAKES

Joel's Bar and Grille is on Main Street, not too far from the firehouse and a few blocks past The Green. A nursery, small shops, the historical society and a pizza place are close by, too. Derek's always thought that its location gives it an intimate neighborhood feel, the way it's within walking distance of so many places. The bar is tucked into a low brick building, and you could almost pass it by without noticing if it weren't for the changing neon signs that management switches up in the front window, depending on the event, the season. They park near The Green and Vera walks beside him with a soft brown scarf tucked into her cropped tweed jacket, brown suede gloves on her hands.

"Wasn't that good?" she asks. "Bella's food is just like homemade."

"Never had a better penne with sausage and peppers. A little wine now, with some nice company, what more could a guy want?"

"Ha, check it out," she says when they get closer to the bar and its red neon Christmas bells blinking on and off as though they're chiming a happy song.

"Getting a jump on the season." Derek opens the door and steps back for her to go in ahead of him. The commotion and festivities inside are infectious, with waitresses stringing silver garland and colored twinkly lights throughout the bar. Another is stacking Christmas records in the old jukebox, and the rock-and-roll carols are already playing.

"Hey guys, we meet again," Samantha says as she pulls her coat on and approaches them. A couple of her friends walk beside her, bundled up and ready to leave. "What's up?" She eyes them with a mischievous grin while pulling her thick black hair from her coat collar.

"Not much," Derek answers. "Just having a drink."

Samantha wraps a wool scarf around her neck and sends a wink their way. "Make it a sweet one!" she says while breezing past, pulling the door open to the cold night.

Derek touches Vera's elbow and points to the raised bar. "Let's grab a seat." He guides her over, saying a quick hello to a few familiar faces as they pass small, square tables clustered beside a dance floor. They sit at the far end of the bar, away from the mounted television where it's a little quieter. "Wine?" he asks her, and when she nods, he orders two glasses.

"I talked to my mom today," Vera tells him as she slips out of her jacket. He takes it from her and drapes it on the back of her stool. "The swelling's gone and her foot's feeling so much better."

"Glad to hear it," Derek says as the bartender sets down their glasses.

"Hey Derek, my man," the bartender greets him. "How's things?"

"What's up, Kevin? I'm hanging in there." Derek takes a sip of the wine. "Busy tonight, no?"

"'Tis the season," Kevin tells him as he moves on to take another order.

The waitresses continue decorating, one draping garland along the half-wall behind them, the other hanging silver and gold ornaments in the greens.

"So my mom? She wanted to stop by and help me clean out the barn this week, but I told her no way. Maybe in a couple weeks, when she can really use her foot easily."

"Better safe than sorry."

"Definitely. But I plan on getting in there tomorrow to sweep it out and toss some old stuff, now that I'm safe from wild animals, thanks to you," she says with a smile, giving his hand a quick squeeze. "You know, catching that beast. Who, I must say, couldn't be more gentle. He's the sweetest barn cat."

"You should probably take him to the vet for shots, keep him healthy."

"Already done. With a clean bill of health. He'll be good company while I'm working in the old Christmas Barn."

"Hang on a second." Derek starts to stand. "Speaking of the barn, I have a little something for you. It was for your housewarming party, but I didn't have a chance to give it to you that night."

"Oh that's so nice, you didn't have to."

"It's out in my truck, let me go get it." He pulls his keys from his pocket. "You'll wait here?"

"Hey, you two." They both look back at Kevin, tending bar and having a few laughs with the patrons. "Holiday cheer's begun," he says while raising an eyebrow and pointing to the mistletoe hanging above them at the bar.

Derek and Vera glance up together at the sprig of mistletoe with a red bow curled around it, and both laugh him off. "No, that's okay," Vera says, a little flustered.

"Just friends, Kev," Derek adds.

"Right, Coop." The bartender crosses his arms in front of him and eyes them until they have to look away from him and at each other.

Derek silently takes his seat on the stool beside Vera and now that he's looking at her, he can't take his eyes off hers. She gives him a small smile and starts to say something, but whatever it is, he doesn't know. Because she stops when he raises his open hand to her neck, touching it alongside her face. "Come here, friend," he whispers as he leans over and kisses her. But it's what happens next that surprises him. Because he thought, really, he'd just keep the bartender quiet and give in, not wanting to hurt Vera's feelings, either. And she starts to pull away, but then it all changes amidst the music and clamor of the bar and he feels her kiss him back, feels her smile beneath his kiss, and when her hand lifts to touch his hand, well, he can't help it really. His other hand rises to cradle her face as he deepens the kiss, his fingers tangling in her thick blonde hair, the moment soft and festive and startling all at once.

"Just friends, like hell," he hears Kevin say under his breath, followed by a low whistle as he turns and heads down the length of the bar.

Derek pulls away then, but not before kissing her again, briefly, once then twice. With his hands cupping her face, she says something softly. "What's that?" he asks, tipping his head to hear her above the talking voices and music rocking the halls with songs of jolly and glasses clinking and chairs and barstools scraping.

"I said," Vera answers, "I guess you gave *him* something to think about."

Derek looks down the bar at Kevin, then stands beside her, his hand moving a strand of hair from her face. "Yeah," he says. "Me, too." He shifts his fleece trail jacket on his shoulders and reaches for a long swallow of his wine. "Come on, it's late. I'll get you home." When she stands, he lifts her coat off her stool and sets it on her shoulders, his arm staying around her as he walks her down around the tables and to the night outside. Okay, and he throws a quick glance back at that darn mistletoe, too.

ten

THE TREES BEYOND HER BARN are stark against the blue sky, their branches bare now. Vera imagines the cove water is just as stark, crystal blue and cold this blustery November morning. That's what she notices when she steps back after hooking her new barn star on the plank of wood right beside the barn doorway—the blue sky stretching above the barn first, then the deep-burgundy-painted barn star. *Every barn needs a star*, Derek told her when he gave her the housewarming gift last night. And now, after a long second standing there admiring it, a second when her fingers reach up to touch the side of her face remembering his mistletoe kiss, she whispers, "Perfect."

A gust of icy wind moves her to open the red-painted door and hurry inside. She needs to make serious progress on getting the space ready for the Marches. The floors had been swept in the past few days, with a particular gray tabby cat chasing after her swooshing broom. The many, many wall shelves were damp-wiped as well. There is no telling how much space the Marches need, but the shelves make for great storage of smaller items.

In the back, a lean-to was once tacked onto the side of the barn. She hasn't ventured in there yet, but with everything else done, that's where she heads now. The door sticks until she puts both hands on the doorknob and wrenches it toward her. "Oh no," she says, reaching up for a string hanging from a bare-bulb light fixture. Boxes upon sealed boxes are stacked, floor-to-ceiling, wall-to-wall. "What the heck?" With her gloved hand, she swipes a layer of dust off one, then wipes it on her old flannel shirt while reading the yellowed shipping label still affixed to it. It's addressed to the Christmas Barn.

"Huh." The box flaps are tucked inside each other, so she pulls them open and takes a look, lifting an envelope left on top and first reading the letter tucked inside. Then, brushing aside crumpled paper in disbelief, she finds a red-and-gold decorative sleigh with a soft layer of artificial snow. "How do you like that?" she asks while lifting it all out and setting it on one of her recently cleaned barn shelves. There's more in the box, off to the side: a lamppost, and pretty little gift boxes festively wrapped, meant to fill the sled.

She pulls another box off the stack and brings it to the center of the barn where the lighting is better, setting it on a small table. This one holds hundreds of dangling gold snowflake ornaments, which she begins to gently hang from random hooks and nails on the walls, and climbing up to the loft, from ceiling beams too. "This can't be." Shining snowflakes glimmer in shafts of dusty sunlight coming in through the paned windows.

But if she's learned anything these past few months, it's that *anything* can be. She can be a local town paper's part-time reporter; she can be the owner of a drafty, historic house; she can watch the skies from her own widow's walk; *and* she can be the proprietor now, apparently, of the complete Christmas Barn inventory left behind and long forgotten.

Another box is filled with an assortment of sleigh bells and she strings a miniature set along the red sleigh on the table, jumping when more bells ring behind her. The big tabby cat is crouched inside the box, pawing at the bells over and over again, sliding them out onto the floor, pouncing on them and filling the barn with a melody of happy jingles.

She slowly turns around, taking in the sight of the few decorations she set out, then laughs when the gold sleigh bells ring again. "Oh those jingles!" she tells the barn cat as his two front paws bat a large bell across the freshly swept floor. "Jingles, jingles, jingles," she says again, smiling as the cat runs past. "I guess you've got a name now."

*

"Holy cow," Brooke says when she arrives with fresh-brewed coffee and a cinnamon coffee cake two hours later. "I am so time travelling." She sets down the food delivery and walks through the barn, her cowboy boots clomping on the floor.

"It's pretty amazing, isn't it?" Vera asks. What started with a few gold snowflakes and one red sleigh has turned into an array of nutcrackers with rosy cheeks and wreaths with red bows and Christmas lanterns and twinkling lights and red-feathered cardinals and Santas and snowmen. "And I haven't even made a dent in the tons of decorations, which are stacked right up to the ceiling."

Brooke walks over to the storage room with Vera standing behind her, peering over her shoulder at the boxed inventory.

"I took out everything you see already just from sheer disbelief," Vera explains. "Don't touch anything, because I'm telling you it's like some sort of Christmas magic takes over and you have to open another, then another."

"Wow!" Brooke looks the room up and down, including the cartons lined against the walls. "The whole Christmas Barn inventory must be in here."

"It seriously is. And check this out." Vera hands her a folded piece of paper. "I found it in an envelope in the first box I opened."

Brooke carefully takes the yellowed paper and they read it together:

Sometimes a place is so special, it becomes a part of who we are. That's what the Christmas Barn did for me. My husband and I owned and operated this place for decades (You may have even stopped in during one Christmas or another), and as I pack up our home here, it's hard to let go. I loved this little New England treasure, tucked into the banks of Addison Cove. But it's time to move on. I'm feeling a little like a migratory goose, heading south now. And there's no room for our Christmas Barn where we're going.

And so … in this back room you'll find all the remaining inventory. Whatever you decide to do with it, I will leave to your discretion. For I feel only you can determine the next chapter, whether that is a new beginning or an end.

Warmly and with many blessings and holiday cheer,
Alice

"You didn't know this was all here when you bought the place?" Brooke asks.

Vera shakes her head. "I guess it was too much to take with her, or to sell off at the time."

"Glory be." Brooke looks at the boxes and few decorations already set out. "It is all so beautiful."

"It is, but seriously, Brooke, what am I going to do with it all?"

"You can't keep it?" Brooke slips out of her quilted riding jacket, leaving a teal scarf around her neck, and heads to the coffee. She hands one to Vera before unwrapping a slice of the cake she'd brought along.

"Keep it?" Vera asks while peeling the lid from her coffee. She takes a sip and looks around, shaking her head. "No, even though Alice might want me to. I have to clean this place out for the Marches. So I'm thinking more like having a huge holiday tag sale with what's in that room. I can definitely use the money, and I'll bet lots of people would like to have some of this. You know, it's sentimental and all, from the Christmas Barn."

"Maybe." Brooke bites into her cake. "Hey," she says then. "Speaking of holidays, I meant to ask you about Thanksgiving. I'm having it at my place this year, on account of Mom's foot. She needs to rest it. So I'm making all the dessert—"

"As if," Vera says around a mouthful of cinnamon cake.

"And my in-laws are making the sides. So I need you to make the turkey."

"Me?"

"Sure. You did it last year, in Boston, and it was so good."

"I guess I could. You must have a portable platter of

some sort, so I can cook it here and bring it with me?"

"Definitely."

"Okay, then," Vera says, sipping her steaming coffee. "That's settled. Wish the rest of this was as easy." She sets down her cup and lifts out pinecone mantel decorations and large gold candles. "Hmm, these would look good right here." She sets them on a narrow shelf that looks like a dark mantel, the candles and pinecones nestled among sprigs of greenery.

Brooke pulls out another box and rips open the flaps, silently lifting out needlepoint stockings and hanging them on nails beneath the mantel shelf. "This stuff's gorgeous," she whispers, then pulls a blue snowflake tree skirt from the bottom of the box, flipping it open with a swoosh as though the flakes are fluttering in the cold November barn air.

eleven

JUST LAST WEEK VERA HUNG a twig-and-berry wreath on her newly stained wood-plank front door. It's hard to believe that the wreath and dried cornstalks and potted mums set around her lamppost will all be put away soon, making way for twinkling lights and garland. But for now, it's Thanksgiving.

She turns on the kitchen television in time for an important steadfast tradition: her father's holiday forecast.

"Snow, snow, snow?" He shakes his head and motions to the clear weather map of the East Coast. "No, no, no." The map widens, showing the entire country. "The sunny morning is custom-made for high school football games across the land," he continues. "But be sure to bring your blankets, and scarves and mittens too. Because it's awfully cold out there. What I *am* predicting is a rushed return to warm houses filled with rattling pots and pans, clinking silverware, and the best part of the holiday … that aroma, oh, that delicious scent of turkey cooking in the oven when you walk in from the cold."

"Wait." Vera sniffs the air in the kitchen. Then she

goes outside to the chilly morning and stops on the front stoop for a minute, rubbing her hands in the cold before walking back inside to sniff again.

Nothing.

She looks at her father wearing his snowflake tie on Thanksgiving, wishing and hoping for a bit of snow, hoping to usher in the Christmas season this weekend with at least a dusting of the white stuff. "Not on the horizon, folks."

She knows what *her* wish is. Vera rushes to her stove to see if it'll come true and pulls open the oven door. The oven into which she slid a turkey on a roasting pan hours ago. A pan that is only lukewarm to the touch. "No way." She looks quickly at the temperature gauge, which is properly set to the right degree, then back at her partially raw, uncooked and more than likely spoiled turkey, before letting the oven door slam shut. Because food-poisoning her family is not an option today, nor any day.

She rushes upstairs—first putting her hand to the bedroom window before throwing on her long, layered silky maxi skirt, ankle boots and bulky fisherman's sweater—and then runs out to the grocery store, which she's sure will be open for only a half day and *isn't* sure she'll get to in time.

Derek stands in front of the small chickens, picking up one, then another, checking their weight. Christmas carols play on the sound system and the store is surprisingly busy.

"You're in luck, we've got two left," he hears the butcher tell a shopper as he carries a large precooked turkey to her cart at the end of the meat case. "Have a nice holiday, now."

Derek considered precooked, but they're too big, so he's settling for a chicken instead.

"Derek?"

He looks up to see Vera approaching with the one-of-two precooked turkeys in her grocery cart. "Vera. You're the precooked?"

"I'm the what?"

"Precooked. I mean, it's just that I heard the butcher …" he says, looking past her shoulder. "Never mind. Hey. Happy Thanksgiving."

"You too!" She glances at the plastic-wrapped chicken sitting beside a bag of carrots and a few potatoes in his cart. "You're not eating alone, are you?"

"Me? No, no." He looks at his paltry food items. "I'm headed over to my sister's later. This is for the weekend. You know, I don't really go for the dried leftovers and her packaged stuffing."

"You're sure? Because there's always room for more at Brooke's, which is where I'm *supposed* to be bringing the turkey, but wouldn't you know it? My oven conked out two hours into roasting the bird. I'm picking up one of these turkeys to-go before I food-poison anyone."

"Wouldn't want that."

"No." She smiles quickly. "Well, Derek. Say hi to Sam for me?"

"I will." He checks his watch. "Hey listen, I've got a few more things to pick up." He motions to his cart.

"Oh! Okay," Vera says with another smile, tipping her head a little as she does. Then she steps around her cart and gives him a hug. "Happy Thanksgiving."

He nods, that's it, just nods when she backs away and

wheels her cart toward the checkout, hiking her large tote up on her shoulder, her long, layered skirt nearly skimming the floor behind her.

※

There's only so long that one can push a piece of pumpkin pie around on a plate, smiling politely and sipping yet another coffee. And after answering one too many questions, repeating one too many *No, I'm not seeing anyone* and *Yes, the house is coming along* and *No, I haven't found full-time work yet* to aunts and cousins and friends at the Thanksgiving table, Vera takes a deep breath and bows out early.

"Hey, Vee," Brooke says when she walks into the kitchen. "That turkey wasn't half bad, dressed up with the trimmings."

"Thanks, sis. I'm glad the store had one left." Vera pushes a wayward chair to the table. "Listen, you don't mind if I cut out, do you?" she asks her sister. "I'll help load the dishwasher before I go."

"I wish I could go with you," Brooke whispers while handing her a plate. "Sneak out and enjoy a little Thanksgiving peace and quiet, maybe take a walk around The Green."

"Vera?" Brooke's mother-in-law calls out. "Oh, Vera!"

"See what I mean?" Brooke asks.

They turn when Brooke's mother-in-law rushes into the kitchen holding a piece of paper. She takes Vera's hand and presses the paper into it. "Before I forget, my cousin works in Rhode Island, at the *Providence Post*. That's his email," she says, nodding to the paper folded in Vera's fingers. "Drop him a line, tell him I sent you. He may have a position available, one better suited to your experience than that part-time work. It's worth a shot, don't you think?"

"Sure, I'll keep it in mind. Thank you so much."

"Glad to help!"

And as Vera settles in her car and buckles her seatbelt and lets the heater warm up before putting the car in gear, she's not sure what exactly would help. Would it help to find a job out of state and have to relocate again? Because maybe she's really liking life right here, right now. She looks up at the snowless sky, at the tiny stars in the black velvet night, stars too far away and tiny to wish on, then drives along Main Street headed toward home. When she passes Cooper Hardware, she's surprised to see the lot illuminated. And when she spots Derek wearing a down vest over a blue flannel shirt and gloves, setting up the Christmas trees, she pulls in.

"Hey stranger, don't you take holidays off?" she asks while getting out of her car and holding her coat closed against the cold.

"Hey there, Vera." He continues lifting balsams and fir trees from a pile and tamping their trunks on the ground before leaning them on the wooden frames set around the parking lot. "Tomorrow's a big day here. Lots of townies decorate this weekend."

"Let me help," Vera says, walking closer.

He looks at her long flowing skirt and shakes his head. "You'll ruin your dress. That's okay, really."

"Well, I'll keep you company, then." When she sees a large carton cut open and stacked with balsam wreaths, she lifts one out and hangs it on the wreath rack. It's cold and they're quiet, but she's not sure if it's because of the cold or something else between them, namely one certain *just-friends* kiss. "These are pretty, Derek, but do you have any bows for them? It'd be nice to dress them up a little."

He looks back at the few wreaths she'd hung and motions for her to wait as he unlocks the hardware store door and goes inside. Minutes later he returns with a couple boxes of ornaments and a few bows. "This work for you?"

"Definitely." She lifts another wreath, nestles frosted gold ornaments within its greens and steps back to take a look.

"How was your dinner?" Derek asks over his shoulder as he straightens an unwieldy tree.

"Oh, the usual. Typical family fare."

"I hear you."

Vera lifts out another wreath and clips on a red velvet bow with a long tail sweeping across it. "You know how it is when you're thirty-four and single at the table, well, the conversation gets prying." She looks over at Derek as he lifts another balsam from the pile and stands it straight, pulling down some of the compressed branches. "That's a pretty one."

Derek leans it against the rail and checks his watch. "Listen, Vera. I've got something cooking on the stove." He hesitates, glancing up at the apartment windows over the hardware store. "Would you like to come in, warm up a little bit?"

Lifting a wreath to the wooden frame, she twists around and looks up at the illuminated second-floor window. "Here? You live here?"

"Upstairs." He puts his hands in his vest pockets and hunches his shoulders against the cold wind that starts gusting. "Come on, you've got to be freezing. Let's go in." He walks over to a door on the side of the building, opens it and looks back, watching her standing at the wreaths, waiting until she sets the wreath down and hurries through the door and up the stairs ahead of him.

He smells the chicken roasting before he even unlocks the door and figures that she does, too. So it can't be more obvious that he'd skipped Sam's turkey dinner and sitting around with the family. It's not like he doesn't see them all every day as it is. Once inside, he puts on another living room light and takes Vera's coat. "Have a seat," he tells her as he heads into the kitchen and pulls the food out of the oven. He gets a large piece of tinfoil and covers the pans on the stovetop, turning to see Vera standing in the doorway.

"Do you need a hand with anything?"

"Vera, no, I'm all set." He looks back at the chicken sitting on the stove. "It's just a little something, well," he says, looking past her, then back at her silently with a long breath.

"Hey," she says after a quiet moment, turning toward the living room, her layered maxi skirt sweeping out behind her. "You should have a tree. A small one. I saw a tiny one outside. I'll go get it?"

"No, no." He follows her back to the living room where it looks like she's already scoping out a spot for that tree. "You wait here where it's warm."

And as he goes outside again, feeling the biting cold and picking up a tree he never planned on having, he glances up at his living room window. Well, a tree won't be enough. So he quickly unlocks the store to get everything else, then hauls it all back up the stairs: tree and stand and boxes of glass ornaments and a string of white twinkling lights.

The thing is, it's not like he'd thought it would be tonight, all this sudden busyness. There's no sadness this time like in other years. No remorse at having a tree, or at the possibility of enjoying the holiday, a remorse he'd felt even this morning. There's just his apartment, he sees it as he walks in with the tiny fir. His apartment with its one brick accent wall; the worn braided rug over hardwood floors; the older sectional sofa and end tables; the large paned windows with no curtains; a framed photograph of Abby in her favorite purple sweater, her brown hair hanging straight, her bangs a little too long, on the console table that Vera stands near, looking up at him as he returns. There's all that and something more. There's a life, somehow, an intensity or purpose in the room that he hasn't felt since Abby's death. And it makes the tree feel suddenly important.

"Okay," he says, pulling off his vest and taking his watch off, too, shaking out his hand as he does. He sets the tree, which can't be more than three feet tall, top to bottom, in the small stand. "What do you think about putting it there?" he asks, motioning to a small mahogany pedestal table in front of the window.

"Perfect," Vera answers, lifting a few books and small lamp out of the way. When he moves the tree there, centering it on the table, she takes a box of ornaments, opens it up and puts a hook on a red one, then holds it aloft, waiting. "You'll need to put on the lights first," she tells him.

"Right." He cuffs his flannel shirtsleeves back over a black thermal shirt beneath, pushes those sleeves up as well, then opens the lights package and lifts out the string of bulbs, plugging it into the wall outlet and lacing the bulbs onto the tree branches.

"I'm keeping you from dinner," Vera says quietly as she picks up another ornament, this one gold, standing close and waiting to hang that one, too.

"That's all right," he answers. "The food's better if it sits awhile." He works the string of lights around the tiny tree.

"If you're sure."

Derek moves beside the tree, glancing at the lot down below outside his window with its own twinkling lights running along the Christmas tree frames. "You don't have somewhere to be on this holiday night, Vera? Not seeing anyone you kept from the Thanksgiving table crowd?"

"No." She steps to the lit tree and hangs the gold ornament, thin bangles on her wrist jingling lightly. "I was dating a coworker in Boston a while back. Bad policy, very bad. He got the promotion, and I got the pink slip and was sent packing. In more ways than one."

"What about the doctor?" he asks while working on a section of lights near the treetop.

"Greg?" She finds a spot for the red ornament. "The guy from when I saw you on my birthday?"

"You were with him at your sister's wedding, too."

"Brooke's?" She squints at him. "Wait a minute. Was that you on the dance floor?"

He shrugs while holding a few of the lights.

"Greg and I are just friends from back in the day. That's all." She smiles and picks up another ornament, touching a few branches while looking for the right place for it. "And what about you, Derek?"

What about him? It's been so long since anyone asked, since anyone didn't look at him with sympathy, that it takes a second to get his thoughts together. He finishes with the white lights, wrapping the end around a branch and tucking it under, then steps back, pushing up his sleeves again. "I was married, for a long time. We met in college in Pennsylvania. Things were okay with us, but they say that a traumatic experience will either bring you closer or split you up. After Abby died, the marriage shifted. We couldn't hold on." He picks up a red ornament. "I don't know. Maybe our daughter was what held us together, and once she was gone …" He pauses, hanging the ornament on the window side of the tree. "Well, it doesn't really matter now. We split up a year after Abby drowned. Sold the house and my ex moved back to Pennsylvania. Her family's there, her home."

"I'm sorry, Derek, about all of it."

"I know. But hey, it's the holidays," he says as he walks over to a small shelf stereo and turns on Christmas carols, "so enough of this sad talk."

"Deal. And if I do say so myself, your tree is looking very festive. Loving the twinkly lights." Vera backs up a step near the window and considers it.

"If you like festive trees," he tells her while hanging a gold ornament near the top, "the store sponsors Addison's Tree Lighting Ceremony on The Green. You'd be amazed at that tree, it'll be lit up and about as festive as Rockefeller Center's." When she doesn't say anything, he looks over at her.

"Will you come with me?" she finally asks while still assessing the tabletop tree.

He looks longer at her standing near the window, but shifting her assessing from the tree to him, as a quiet song about home and Christmas and missing someone plays on the stereo.

"Come on," she persists, walking to the tree while holding an ornament. "It'll be fun! We'll bring hot chocolate, sing a few songs." She lifts a small branch near where he stands and he puts his hand on hers to stop it from fussing, feeling her delicate gold bracelets move beneath his touch.

"Vera." He takes the glass ornament from her hand and sets it on the table.

"But we're not done," she answers softly.

He reaches over and turns off a tabletop lamp so that only the white twinkling lights of the tree illuminate the small room. Then he takes her hand again and leads her to the dark green sofa and motions toward it. "Just sit," he says so quietly, he wonders if she hears him. With his hands on his hips, he drops his head with a long breath, then sits with her and leans back and eyes the decorated tree.

She sighs beside him. "It's so pretty. I love it when a tree lights a room."

A few moments pass, time that is purely Christmas with its peace, before Derek answers, "Me, too." He reaches his arm around her shoulder and they just sit in his hardware store apartment and look at the tree together. That's it, nothing else, because it's enough. It's what the whole day led to—with all the running around and holiday mood and people and talking and last-minute grocery shopping and tree-and-wreath set-up in the store lot and chicken cooking and Vera. This. She shifts close and his hand touches her hair while they sit in the light of that tree. "I waxed the store sled today." He feels her head turn as she watches him talk. But his eyes stay on the tree, his hand touching her soft blonde hair. "It was sunny earlier and it felt good to be outside, even in the cold."

"People must love that, taking a sleigh ride."

"It's a pretty sled, you'd like it. Red, with a green velvet seat. And lots of shiny gold trim. Gold runners, too."

"Sounds very merry." She settles close into his arm and looks at the lights on the small tree.

"I never would have had a tree this year," he says, and a few more moments pass, the kind when you do nothing but look at tiny lights sparkling in boughs of green, which is actually everything. "So thank you, Vera."

"For this?" she asks, sitting up a little and turning her face to his.

His hand pulls her closer and he kisses her in the dimly lit room, the twinkling lights and low music and shadows all a part of the tenderness of the kiss.

But three loud knocks that shouldn't be a part of it, suddenly are. Three sharp knocks followed by Sam's voice. "Derek?" she asks as she opens his unlocked apartment door.

Vera stands right away, smoothing her skirt, while Derek sits back straight on the sofa and clears his throat. "What is it, Sam?" he asks as he slowly stands.

"I brought food," she says, rattling two large bags of plastic containers while rushing into the kitchen. "Turkey, my homemade stuffing, mashed potatoes, pumpkin pie, the works." After a quiet second, she calls out from the kitchen, "I don't know why you cooked a chicken. Didn't you figure I'd drop this off?" When she walks through the kitchen door, she stops in her tracks right as Derek turns on a lamp and Vera is slipping into her coat. "Oh! I guess not." Her eyes shift from Vera to the tree to Derek. "Well, why didn't you say something, Derek?"

"I was just leaving," Vera says.

"You don't have to go," he tells her quietly. "Sam's not staying long."

"No, really. I've got an early day tomorrow. My Holly Trolley tour is scheduled. For the article?"

He nods, then turns to his sister.

"Well, happy Thanksgiving, Vera! It's good to see you again." Sam walks over and gives Vera a hug. "And great tree going on here." With a slightly raised eyebrow, she turns to Derek. "So this is why you backed out of my turkey dinner?"

Vera looks quickly from Derek and back to Sam. "No," she explains, rushing to the chair to pick up her large tote. "No, really. I just stopped by on my way home, and well, the tree," she turns and smiles at the tree, then looks at Derek with a shrug that says *Get me out of this?*

He walks to her and kisses the side of her face. "Let me see your phone."

"My phone?" She reaches into her tote and hands it to him.

"Give me a ring when you get home," he says while programming in his number. "So I know you made it okay."

She nods slightly, looks to Samantha with a wave, hikes up her tote and hurries toward the door with Derek following close behind to walk her out. "Oh, Derek," she says, turning back so quickly he nearly bumps into her.

"What is it?" he says softly, taking her hands for a second.

"I almost forgot. Well. It's just that I'm having this painting thing Saturday. You know, Brooke and Brett are coming over for pizza and painting."

"Painting what?"

"My dining room. So anyway, it would be great if you could come, too. You know, a painting party. Food, drinks, a few laughs. And I promise I'll be there this time."

He nods, watching her closely.

"So you'll come? After work?"

"You bet."

twelve

IT'S A CHRISTMAS VILLAGE COME to life. That's what Vera jots down in her notes when the trolley passes Wedding Wishes with its twinkly lights strung around the windows and the bride mannequin wearing a white fur cloak over her long white gown. And there's Whole Latte Life with its pieces of cotton tucked into the window corners to look like snow, the coffee shop enticing you in for a holiday mocha. On The Green, fresh balsam garland wraps up the coach light lampposts topped with festive wreaths, and beyond, the covered bridge is outlined in white glimmering lights. Really, how many times has she seen these quaint scenes set out in storefronts decorated with miniature holiday villages, or in a friend's home—the white-steepled chapel and nursery with its poinsettia greenhouse and historic colonial figurines set along a fireplace mantel, or in a dining room china cabinet?

Yes, Addison looks like a full-size ceramic Christmas village with swags of evergreen garland across white picket fences, pine wreaths on doors, candles in the windows. And as the green-and-gold trolley with its jingling bells drives through town, women smile as they hurry past with bags of gifts; neighbors stop and turn as they string lights on their shrubs; and carolers outside Sycamore Square sing a merry tune while bedecked in scarves, caps and mittens. She waves at them as the trolley drives by, thinking the only thing missing is snow.

There's a change, though, as they reach the neighborhood near the cove that includes her Dutch colonial. The large old homes, with their painted wood shutters and widow's walks and occasional carriage houses set beneath even taller oak and maple trees on imposing yards, have no holiday spirit. Windows framed in antique lace are dark, grand wood-panel front doors bare. Not a balsam wreath is found, not a window-candle lit nor a mechanical snowman waving hello. Nothing.

"It's been quiet on that one stretch for years," the trolley driver explains when she questions him. "Ever since that little girl died, so close by. Folks just never seemed to find it in their hearts to decorate there since."

❧

Derek's been seeing the Holly Trolley jingle past the hardware store all morning. Whether he's at the checkout, or in the tree lot, or helping a customer out on the floor, it catches his eye and has him do a double take, the green vehicle toodling by with its gold top and gold scrollwork, a wreath hung on the front grill.

So it's no wonder that he notices when it stops in front of the store to let a few riders off, Vera being one of them. She steps down wearing a short black cape over black skinny slacks and black knee-high boots, with bright green leather gloves on her hands. The trolley's a far cry from the big news stories of Boston, but it's so apparent that Vera gives every story the same professional treatment. She turns back to say a few words to the trolley driver, finishing up her tour and interview, then slips a notepad into her tote and heads over to the Christmas tree lot. Derek lifts his cargo vest off the hook behind the counter and goes out to see her.

"Can I help you, ma'am?" he asks with a wink, Zeus following at his side, wagging his tail in a slow loop.

She smiles at them. "Well, sir," she begins, "it depends on how much you know about these here Christmas trees."

By that time he's at her side, takes her shoulders lightly and gives her a quick kiss. "Hey, Vera. How was the trolley?" he asks, holding her gloved hands in his.

"So charming. What a pretty town this is, I wish you could've come on the tour, too."

"Maybe another time," he says, turning to the tree display. "Now, about that tree."

Vera walks the length of the first line of balsams, studying them carefully.

"See one you like?"

"How about that one?" she asks, pointing to a large tree on the end.

Derek lifts it off the tree frame and tamps the stump so that the green branches nicely fall open. "Zeus!" he calls out when the dog veers off toward a small family. "Come on," he orders, reaching into his pocket for a small dog biscuit.

"He's very friendly, in his kingdom and all."

Derek looks down at the yellow lab sitting at his feet beside the balsam fir he's holding. "Sometimes I think he's still looking for Abby." He nods over to the family

Zeus was following, one with a young girl. "She loved this old mutt. When I'd bring her to the store, she'd set up her toys on the window ledge inside and the dog would lay right there with her. Part of *her* kingdom, I guess." He pats the dog's big head.

"That's so sweet," Vera says with a smile.

"Now what about this tree?" He gives the tree a small shake. "Sweet for you?"

"No." Vera eyes it closely. "Wrong shape."

So he sets it back and hands Zeus his treat.

"Maybe that one," she says in the second row, and he pulls up a smaller blue spruce and tamps that one, too. "Way too small."

They continue walking along the trees, passing other couples and families who are standing random trees straight up; setting Scotch pines back down; stopping, backtracking; doing needle-checks on a white spruce; looking at balsams from a distance, then close-up.

Derek steers her to the next row where the trees are taller. "You've got a big, grand house, Vera. You need a tree that makes a statement, don't you think?"

"Hmm." She walks slowly, her hands touching this one, pointing to that one, waving off wrong ones. "How do you know?" she finally asks. "How will I know which one is *thee* tree for me?"

Several customers wait to have their trees checked out, then wrapped in netting and tied onto their cars. "Listen," he says, standing close beside her. "You'll just know. After years of doing this, I see it all the time. The tree will, well, it'll just *speak* to you. You know," he says, pointing to the small decorated tree in the second-floor window, its lights on and twinkling brightly, even in broad daylight. "Like mine did." He pulls heavy work gloves from his vest pocket. "I've got to run. I'll catch up with you tomorrow night. Do you need paint? Any brushes?"

"No," she says, distracted by all the trees as she walks slowly among them. "I'm good."

With Zeus still at his heels, Derek hurries to the netting area, looking over to see Vera consider a few more Christmas trees before leaving with only a balsam wreath decorated with pinecones and holly berries and a burgundy velvet bow, still not hearing the call of her tree.

thirteen

I TOLD YOU THIS COLOR would be nice," Brooke says as she rolls a swath of the deep gold paint on Vera's dining room wall. An extra paintbrush is tucked in the back pocket of her overalls.

"And as usual, you're right," Vera answers. She ties a bandana over her hair while looking at Brooke's sample. "It's amazing how it warms the room right up."

"I researched the colors for the time period of this house and saw lots of these golds and ambers." Brooke paints another strip of gold. "Can't you picture the old colonial family gatherings and dinner parties here? And with that view of the cove, wow, you wouldn't want to leave this room, whether it's the 1800s or today."

"Maybe it's because so much time was spent at sea. The ship captains sailed all over the world and when they returned from the cold, stormy seas, they came home to warmth and comfort. Thus the gold paint."

Brett stands high up on a ladder in jeans and an old college sweatshirt, and lines a strip of blue tape along the crown molding, having worked his way around the room.

"Hey Vera, where's your new dude?" he asks.

"Derek?" She dips a brush into the paint can and edges the color along the doorway's white molding.

"Yeah, I need another guy here before Brooke gets me in the kitchen with oven mitts on, and makes me help with dinner."

"Ha! Is it really Derek you want here, or the pizza he's picking up for me?"

"It's always about the food, Vee," Brooke reminds her. "Don't ever forget that. If you guys ever fight, or don't see eye to eye, or whatever. Just bring on the food and you'll work it out."

When there's a knock at the side door, Vera rushes through the kitchen. "The natives are restless," she tells Derek while holding the door open as he carries in two large pizza boxes, kissing her hello on the way. A cold wind blows in with him and she quickly shuts the door. "I opened a folding table in the dining room for Brett. As long as he can eat and paint at the same time, we'll keep him happy."

Derek puts down the pizza, then checks out the paint color while rolling up his olive-plaid flannel shirt cuffs. "Hmm. Something's missing."

"Really?" Vera asks. "You don't like the color?"

"I love the color. Hang on, let me get something from my truck."

"All right!" Brett tells him when Derek returns with a radio. "Tunes."

"Yup. Can't paint without the right atmosphere."

Derek takes off his down vest and plugs in an old construction-site radio covered in paint splatters, the antenna slightly bent. The tuning dial is a little loose, too, but as soon as the music begins, Vera sees that all that matters is the sound. Paintbrushes are dipped with more finesse, Brett brings a little style to rolling gold on the far wall, and Brooke gets artistic, doing a two-step with her technique.

"Nice," Vera tells her when she finishes painting a gold heart around her and Brett's names on the wall between two large windows. "I think I'll leave that right there."

"Hey, anyone delivering pizza up here?" Derek asks from the top of the ladder while painting around the crown molding.

"I'm on it, special delivery just for you." Vera hands him a plate loaded with a sausage-and-pepperoni slice.

He sets his brush across the top of the paint can on the ladder tray and bites into the pizza. "This is a great room, Vera, those are some cool built-ins," he says, pointing to a china cabinet along the wall.

Brett walks into the room carrying two bottles of beer. "Hey guy, how about a brew?"

"Definitely," Derek says, taking one from him and setting it on the top of the ladder. "I remember when Abby helped me paint the house one time."

"Man, you let a kid paint your house?" Brett asks.

"Shit, she was out there for hours, her little arm painting away."

"Aw, that's cute." Brooke stops to listen. "Daddy's helper?"

"I was up on the ladder just like this, and she was down below helping me out." He takes a drink of the beer and says over his shoulder to Brett, "With her own paintbrush and a bucket of *water.*"

"Well, that's different then," Brett answers while rolling paint. "Saved you from doing any touch-up, anyway."

And Vera sees how Derek's purely in the memory, and it's okay. Because that's the kind of easy night it is.

As the music plays on, a classic rock number bridges Vera's historic house to the present, and what she pictures is this: a parlor party from more than a hundred years back, maybe with guests in formal clothes, long dresses and such, listening to phonograph records on a crank-up Victrola. That happens sometimes—when she steps into a musty closet, or when she beats the old Oriental rug outside on the clothesline, the dust rising from it, or when she hears a step on the staircase creak—she envisions what life was like in this big house many, many years ago.

Brooke pours more of the gold paint into her tray. "Uh-oh. Jingles, scat!" She shoos the cat as he sniffs the paint, leaving a dot of gold clinging to a whisker. "Move along, kitty." He sits for a second surveying the paint mess in the room before walking to the pizza table and settling beneath it. "That's right, you supervise from over there."

And if that's the case, if Jingles is supervising, Vera thinks he does a pretty good job of it. Because doesn't her house take on a new life as the dining room walls are covered with their gold hue, a few drinks and hearty laughs spicing up the color and bringing cheer to the big old room. If only echoes of this night would ring into any dinner served here in the days and months to come, she'd love it. And when they're done painting, and eating, and, okay, dabbing paint strokes onto each other's jeans in an impromptu game of *Got You Last,* either the magic of the music or the magic of people who know you best kicks in.

"You've got the perfect hardwood floors to christen this room with a dance, Vee." Brooke moves aside the ladder and scoops up the drop cloths, then looks at Brett. "Maestro?"

Brett flips through the stations on Derek's paint-spattered radio until he finds the right country music, cranks it up and then moves beside Brooke. On just the right beat, they revisit their wedding night and glide right into the Electric Slide, clapping and stomping through the dance steps with happy ease.

Vera watches them from the arched doorway, her arms crossed in front of her, grinning at it all until she looks over to see Derek silently point first to her, then to himself. And once they join in, she doesn't know if there ever was a happier sound in her historic Dutch colonial. Heck, she's not even sure the sea captain's boots walking through the heavy front door after a long voyage could top the sound of Brett's and Derek's work boots on the wood floor, along with Brooke's heel-tapping cowboy boots and Vera's blue lace-up sneakers, all dancing up a storm on hundred-year-old planks of oak beneath them, tapping, kicking and spinning the room right into present day.

❧

Derek grabs another slice of pizza and walks into the living room to see Brett holding a marshmallow over the fireplace flame, drinking a beer as he does, while Brooke waits beside him with her graham cracker and piece of chocolate.

"Here you go," Brett tells her as he sets the melting marshmallow on her cracker.

"All right!" Brooke whispers. "Love these." She takes a bite of the s'more and closes her eyes. "Heaven on a cracker. Want some?" she asks around the food, holding her s'more out for Brett to sample.

Derek finishes his slice of pizza and sits on the couch. "Let me get that," he says a moment later, starting to stand when Vera carefully slides a beanbag chair down her staircase.

"No, sit, sit! I'm good. Listen, I don't have too much furniture yet, guys." She pushes the chair over near the TV, then sinks on the sofa beside Derek. "So if someone wants to get comfortable on this, be my guest."

"Here." Brooke hands her a s'more of her own. "They're delicious."

Vera holds it up to Derek and when he takes a bite, he sees. He sees how life goes on, and how easy it is to not realize it, especially when tragedy takes hold. But it does go on, and the only way to know it is to step out of the tragedy, and it feels like pushing open a heavy, mysterious curtain and walking right into the rest of the world. Head on.

"Hey, Lauren called me today, Brooke," Vera says. "She got the article I'd sent along, and we got to talking. I guess she spent a lot of time at Stony Point last summer, and I was thinking—"

"Wait! Let me guess," Brooke interrupts. "We should rent a cottage together?"

Vera laughs. "Yes! Gosh, it's been so long since we've been to the beach. Would you guys be game?"

"I could go for some fun in the sun," Brett answers, finishing his beer and getting comfortable in the beanbag chair. "But it's impossible to even believe it'll be summer again the way that wind is howling tonight."

Derek puts his arm around Vera's shoulder and watches the fire crackling in the big brick fireplace, taking it all in. Talk and good food and summer plans. Really, at this one moment it seems like just enough.

"And you're coming, too," Vera whispers to him.

Derek kisses the side of her head and at the same time his cell phone rings. "It's Kevin," he says when he checks it. "Let me take this, it's about the boats." He stands and heads into the dining room, talking briefly with Kevin about a friend who wants to join the procession. They estimate details on boat size and type, and where it'll fit in the lineup. "Want to clean up these paint trays now?" he calls out when he's done.

"No!" Brooke and Vera insist together.

"We're starting the Christmas movie marathon. Get back in here and have a marshmallow. Or pizza," Vera says. And when he walks back into the room, watching her, she adds, "Or just sit with me."

And he does. He just sits and lets time unfold on Vera starting the movie and setting the remote down on the coffee table. Unfold on Brooke fussing with another s'more while Brett starts dozing on the beanbag chair. The room is warm, the lights are dim, the firewood sparks and snaps. And right when the movie starts, Jingles quietly walks in.

"Wait," Vera whispers while squinting at the cat. "No way." She leans forward on the couch and stares at the floor over in the direction he came from. "Jingles!" she calls out while jumping quickly to her feet.

Derek looks; they all do, actually. Even Brett sits up at the sound of Vera's exasperated voice. And they all see it at the same time, too. They see the trail of wet, gold paw prints crossing the wooden dining room floor, fading to a lighter gold where the cat sauntered into the living room before scampering out to the kitchen.

fourteen

VERA LIFTS THE TABLETOP CAROUSEL from the box in the storage room and gasps at her find. How many Decembers did her mother bring her to the Christmas Barn all those years ago? The family tradition was to find a new ornament for their tree; but for Vera, it was to visit these magical Christmas swans. She'd walk through the big old barn with all its festive holiday décor until she found them. Because she'd seen swans before, in the salt marsh at Stony Point, and loved to watch them. That's why these birds drew her, the glimmering, sparkling carousel swans spinning slowly around a painted scene of three ships. One swan would slide past, then another, each neck gracefully arched with a small balsam wreath and red bow decorating them elegantly.

And that's where she'd stay until she felt her mother's touch on her back, felt her breath as she bent low to tell Vera how pretty the carousel birds were, that the white sparkles looked like snow on their feathers. And they'd watch the swans together until her mother took her mittened hand and finally led her through the store to leave, holding a red shopping bag with a new ornament inside.

Memories, life, they're one and the same. Because Vera holds the carousel up now and what she remembers is this: Being that young girl with silky blonde hair falling across her blue wool coat, her head turned back, her eyes still watching the swans peacefully swimming, swimming, around and around and around the sea, forever beautiful, forever suggesting something she didn't know then, but maybe sensed, about the eternal rhythms of the sea, and of life.

She opens a slip of paper tucked in with the carousel. *Not For Sale* is handwritten across it, underlined twice. *For Children's Display Only!* So the previous owner understood how important the swans were. If she'd kept it just for Vera, she'll never know. But looking at them now brings her again to the edge of the sea, to a simple peace conveyed by the white birds.

Until a loud jangling bell reminds her exactly where she actually is and what she's doing as Jingles knocks over a small box from a tabletop, jumps down and soccer-pats a sleigh bell across the wide boards of the barn floor. He's a blur of soft, fluffy motion that nearly trips her sister when she walks in with two large boxes tied closed with a thin piece of string.

"Oh! Jingles, you rascal!" Brooke says to the cat. "You scared the daylights out of me."

Vera picks up the swan carousel and gently sets it back in its box.

"Yoo-hoo!" Brooke calls out. "Vera?"

"Back here," Vera answers, walking out of the storage room.

Brooke sets her boxes on the old checkout countertop

near the door and begins opening them. "I'm glad I caught you. The library bake sale is this weekend and you have to sample these and tell me which ones to make."

Vera looks into the boxes laden with jam-filled coffee-cake muffins, some strawberry, some raspberry, blueberry, and peach. "For the love of muffins, why oh why are you tempting me like this? I'll put on ten pounds."

"Well, don't have them all at once." She sets out a couple muffins on a napkin on the counter. "I wanted to drop them off for you on my way to work. Maybe you can bring some to Mom's later on?"

"I'm really pressed for time, Brooke, so I can't promise anything. I'm working on an extended profile piece and have to interview the fire marshal."

"Another article? That's good news, Vera!"

"Except there's lots of research with this one, keeping me super busy. I can maybe swing by Mom's after the interview, for a few minutes anyway." Temptation gets the best of her, convincing her to pick up an overloaded muffin and take a big bite. "Mmm, these are sinful," she says, wiping a smear of jam from the corner of her mouth. "I swear, if you'd bring these in to Tom's, you know, and sell them in the reception area, your boss would be the most popular lawyer in Addison."

"I wish. But unfortunately in the real world, I'm a paralegal, not a baker." Brooke takes a muffin covered with drizzles of raspberry jam and bites into it, saying around the food, "But let me tell you, if I could find a way to bake like this all the time …" She glances around the space filling up with artificial Christmas trees and snow villages and eight sparkling reindeer and twinkling lights winding up the banister to the loft where a mechanical, life-size pair of carolers stands, their mouths in a permanent O-shape as they look from sheet music in their hands and then up to the heavens in imagined song. "Well, baking full-time would feel like Christmas, *all* the time." Brooke sighs and stuffs the rest of her muffin in her mouth. "Got to run," she says then. "I'm so late for work."

"Here, take a couple of these. That way Tom won't be mad."

"Good thinking." Brooke closes up one of the boxes just as Jingles runs across the floor after a sliding bell. She pulls her car keys from her purse, glancing after the cat, then surveying the whole barn. "It's amazing how festive this place is looking."

Vera knows exactly what her sister means. Because what Vera's been thinking lately is that the barn, filled with its Christmas displays, looks more like the North Pole, or Santa's workshop, than a tag sale. Ornaments hang on the trees, wreaths line the wall behind the checkout counter, silver spray-painted pinecones fill crystal vases. Then she looks at the muffins set out on the counter, sitting on pretty scalloped napkins.

"You know, Brooke, would you ever consider selling coffee cakes at my tag sale? Christmas coffee cakes, maybe? I'll bet they'd go over really well."

Brooke eyes Vera, eyes her bakery box, then looks out at the Christmas wonderland taking shape in the barn. "Now that's not a bad idea."

fifteen

"CONNECTICUT WAS THE FIRST NEW England state to make Christmas a legal holiday. And from the crowd here, I can see why," Santa Claus calls into a microphone near the unlit tree. "Addison's Christmas spirit just fills me with joy. Ho, ho, ho!"

Derek keeps an eye out for Vera, meeting him here after he closed up the store. The maple tree trunks and branches along the edge of The Green are wrapped in white twinkling lights, casting a soft glow in the dark night. They light up smiling faces and brightly colored caps and scarves and mittened hands cupping hot drinks. When he sees her waving to him from across the lawn, he hurries over.

"You know who that Santa is, don't you?" Derek says into Vera's ear, leaning down close.

Vera looks out at the Santa Claus standing beside the high school band tuning up for a Christmas concert. "No."

She looks up at Derek, and he can't help it. He gently brushes a strand of hair off her face, his hand touching her fluffy earmuffs, then reaches behind her neck as he gives her a quick kiss. "Don't let on to any of the kids here. It's my father."

"No way!"

Vera walks closer to the tree-lighting festivities, squeezing through the crowd until they have a front-row view. People bundled in warm coats press close around them and Derek stands behind her, wrapping his arms around her waist.

"Christmas trees take about seven to ten years to mature," Santa continues to the crowd. "Judging from the size of this grand tree," he continues, leaning back and looking up toward the top of a dark unlit tree looking like only a shadow in the night, "I'd say Addison knows how to grow 'em, regardless of how many years it's been here!"

Applause breaks out from the families all looking up at the towering pine tree.

"Cold?" Derek asks over her shoulder when he feels Vera shiver in her red buffalo-plaid pea coat and white mittens covered with sequined snowflakes, cupping a steaming hot chocolate.

"A little." She takes a sip of the drink. "Want some?" He takes the cup for a quick taste. "Your dad makes a great Santa," she says while he does.

In front of them, his father leads the crowd in a verse of *Jingle Bells*. "They're playing your cat's theme song," he tells Vera, and she laughs, swaying slightly to the music.

A man beside Derek lifts his young daughter onto his shoulders to give her a better view of Santa and the hardware store sleigh brought in for the festivities. The sleigh is filled with wrapped presents next to a long line of children waiting to have their picture taken on it with Santa.

"Hey, is that your sleigh?" Vera asks him over her shoulder.

Derek nods. "Dad always loved playing Santa on Christmas Eve," he says when his father sits in the sleigh and a young girl climbs up to have her picture taken. "He'd come over to the house in full costume and Abby never suspected it was him."

As he talks, Vera leans back into his arms, listening closely to Derek over the other voices and the high school band playing a familiar carol.

"She'd be in her pajamas already and get real quiet," he goes on, bending low to Vera's ear, feeling her soft hair against his cheek while watching the girl sitting with his father turn her face up, wide-eyed. Derek knows that expression; he'd seen it on his daughter's face, too. And it's funny how it happens then, how he envies his own father, who might be seeing a little bit of Abby, still, in the awe in these kids' faces. "And her eyes, man, they lit up. They just sparkled." He takes a breath and shifts his stance, his arms still around Vera's waist. "Abby and my dad sat in a big chair near our tree," he says, watching his father now waving at the children nearby, "and he'd ask her if she'd been good all year." He stops then, not really able to say more. Because what can he say? Everything, and yet nothing.

Vera turns to him, brushes her mitten across his cheek and waits.

"The last time I was here, it was the year Abby died. And she sat up on my shoulders to see the view. Like the girl over there." He hitches his head to the right and Vera looks over and smiles sadly.

"Aw, Derek. I'll bet she loved that."

"What I wouldn't do to have a few more of those moments."

"You always will have them, though, with your own

memories. Because isn't that what life is? It's all memories, when you really think about it."

He looks past her to his father and the sea of families and faces, all softly illuminated and so excited for what's to come as they watch the shadowy tree on The Green. Something about their hope and laughter and the twinkling maple tree branches on the outskirts seem to make the darkness all the more noticeable. He wonders how much longer until the tree is lit, pulling away from Vera to check his watch. It's so cold out tonight, and the cold has a way of making the dark look even darker.

"Ten! Nine!" The tree-lighting countdown begins, led by Santa.

The crowd chants along, "Eight! Seven!"

Vera takes Derek's hand, but there's an urgency to the countdown as the moments of darkness and cold tick away with each second and he knows that for everyone here, the darkness and cold will end in seconds. The magnificent light of Christmas will erase it all.

"I'm sorry, Vera. I can't do this." He pulls away and quickly pushes through a swarm of families. She calls out his name, only once. *Derek!* The concern in her voice almost stops him, almost, but he keeps walking through the crowd, thinking it was wrong to come here, to meet Vera for the festivities. Because in too many faces, in too many moments, he still sees Abby.

Vera notices a car pulling up to the curb as the crowd thins. She squints into the darkness, looking around a family hurrying past in the cold. "Greg?" she asks, stepping closer.

"Hey," he says, parking and getting out. He wears a long dark coat and leather gloves. "It's good to see you."

"You, too." She wraps her arms around the waist of her pea coat. "Brrr, what a cold night. Did you catch the tree lighting?"

"No. I just got off the evening shift. Over at the hospital."

She nods.

"Would you like to get a drink, maybe? Or a coffee somewhere?"

"Oh, no. I'm here, well, I *was* here with Derek. Derek Cooper. Something came up and he had to leave early."

Greg looks past her shoulder, as though he'll see him. Or as though giving her a chance to say more. And so she does. "I'm kind of seeing him now. Derek."

He looks at her again, stepping closer. "He's a lucky guy, then." He takes one of her mittened hands in both of his. "Can I at least give you a ride home?"

"Oh! No, that's okay. My car's close by, I was just headed there now." She points to her car parked near his. "There was an emergency, sort of. And Derek had to leave," she finds herself explaining again. And it was an emergency, she's sure. She's sure he didn't plan on whatever beautiful Christmas memories he has of sweet Abby tormenting him tonight, seeing all the other children still here, still happy, still with their families. "So anyway, thanks Greg."

"Well listen," he tells her, backing up a step. "You have a nice Christmas, if I don't see you before then."

She nods quickly.

"Hey, how's your mom's foot?"

"So much better! I'll tell her you asked for her."

He grasps her arms. "Merry Christmas, Vera," he says

113

quietly, giving her a kiss on her cheek. "Come on, I'll walk you to your car."

When she gets in, Vera waves goodbye to Greg and lets the car engine warm up for a couple minutes. She sits with her hands clasped, holding them to her chilled face. The sky outside her windshield is vast tonight. It always seems that way, so much more expansive on bitter cold nights. Tiny, tiny stars sparkle far, far above, too far away to lighten the winter sky. They look like the tiniest of snowflakes just waiting to fall. There's not a cloud in sight to help, either, to bring a soft hue to the night.

Her father's been searching for snow clouds for weeks now, eager for that first, sweet snowfall. She leans forward and looks up to the clear night sky. One day soon, those clouds will roll in, heavy with precipitation that will fall gently to the earth, little winter stars tumbling down from the clouds, spinning and blowing, changing shape dramatically during the course of one snowstorm.

Vera waits in her car, just in case. Maybe she'll see Derek on the outskirts. Maybe he needs some space, that's all, to think about Abby in a different way now, one he can cherish instead of resist. Maybe he needs to be alone to find her in his own personal way at Christmastime.

Finally, she puts her car in gear and pulls out of the parking space near The Green. The town tree is so pretty, twinkling in the night, and it breaks her heart that Derek couldn't stay. That he couldn't see the light of it. The Green is quiet now; the families who sang along with the high school band, took happy pictures and strolled in the cold had finally made their way home.

She glances back at the tree sparkling brightly in the night, then drives toward Cooper Hardware. Her eyes spot the building from a block away. The Christmas tree lot is strung with small lights, the balsam and white pine and spruce trees propped up in the cold, but the lot is empty. Dim lights are on in Derek's apartment above, but whether or not he's home, she can't tell. The little window-tree they decorated together is dark tonight.

It all makes her worry as she sees Derek struggle to come to grips with one long-ago horrible day. Because what it seems like is this: He's still falling through that dark cloud, still tumbling and faltering as his life changes shape dramatically during the course of one ongoing storm.

sixteen

VERA HOLDS THREE WREATH BOWS, one plaid, one gold satin and one burgundy velvet. There's just enough space on the barn beam to pin these on, leaving the wooden beam completely covered in bows of all shapes and styles: candy-cane striped and gold-edged velvet, eight-loops and fifteen-loops, sparkled sheer and country plaids, two tails and four, and her favorite, blue-and-white snowflake patterned.

She steps onto a footstool to hang the very last one high up on the beam and sees the nearby wall of shelves lined with every type of Christmas star imaginable, including winter stars of silver and gold in the snowflake ornaments. An idea comes to her then, a little sales promotion for her tag sale. She'll offer shoppers her own version of Buy One Get One Free: Buy one star ornament, either real star or snowflake winter star, and get one *wish* free. Because shouldn't every star come with a wish?

"Knock, knock!"

"Mom?" Vera moves carefully off the step stool.

"Hi, honey." Her mother closes the barn's red door behind her, but not before a draft of icy air blows in. "I'm here to pick up that music box."

"Music box?" Vera walks over to the doorway and takes her mother's coat.

"For the toy drive at the TV station, remember? It's today. Dad and I are dropping off a bag of goodies."

"Oh, the teddy bear music box. It's right there," she points further down the counter. "Near the door."

Her mother pulls off her gloves, one finger at a time, while looking around the barn's interior. "Oh my God! Would you look at this place?"

Vera realizes that her mother hasn't been to the barn in weeks. With her astonishment at its Christmas transformation—at its pinecone reindeer and squirrels, its needlepoint stockings, its old horse stall decorated with gold garland around the half-open top—well, her mother's stunned reaction clues Vera in to the wonderland the barn has since become.

"This is just beautiful, Vera. Dazzling!" She stops at the wreath-bow beam and looks it up and down, smiling. "Can I help? I'd love to put out some of the old Christmas Barn decorations too. Be a part of the history." She turns to Vera with an expectant glimmer in her eyes.

Vera smiles in disbelief because there it is *again*, that magic that overcomes people when they step into the barn now. With Brooke, it's gotten out of control as she methodically builds a Christmas village whenever she's here, spellbound with adding pine trees and antique coach lights and glittering snow to her festive tabletop town.

"Where's Dad?" Vera asks as her mother walks around, lightly touching glittering ornaments and sighing at wintry displays.

117

"He let himself into the house and went straight up to your widow's walk. There's a change in the air that he's certain means snow and he wants to see the clouds from that vantage point."

"I'll go say hi to him." She eyes her mother, who is still entranced by the barn. "Listen, Mom. I have so many boxes of ornaments but no more artificial trees to hang them on. Do you have any idea what I can do with them? I'd hang them from the ceiling beams, but I've got the gold snowflakes up there."

Her mother looks up at the gilded, delicate constellation hanging from above. "Wow." And then she spots a shelf of old clay flowerpots stacked right below the loft area. "What about those?"

"The pots?"

"They'll be so pretty! Point me to the ornaments and I'll stack some in the clay pots, add a little baby's breath and cotton snow and voilà!"

"You sure you're okay on your feet now?"

"Of course, it was only a sprain. Go on up and see your dad and I'll deck the pots with balls of jolly."

And quicker than Vera can say *Fa la la la la*, her mother's digging into a new box of green-and-gold striped ornaments.

❧

"Lots of blue sky out there," Vera says as she climbs onto her widow's walk. The early afternoon sky is royal blue, with high wispy white clouds moving across it. "Fair weather, Dad?"

"For now," he answers, leaning on the railing facing the cove. "Those are cirrus clouds, Vee. And they *can* be a signal that the weather's about to change."

Vera moves beside her father, pulls her thick cardigan close and leans on the railing, too. "They're pretty, that's for sure." They watch the early December sky over the water for a moment before Vera continues. "The view alone was worth buying this property for. I never get tired of it."

"You're looking at one of nature's best canvases. Because let's face it, sights like this one here have inspired the great masters."

"Now there's an idea. Maybe someday I'll set up an easel and try my hand at painting. In my spare time," she adds with a wink. "I've been so busy lately, with work and now the barn, too."

"And how about that doctor, Vee? Have you been seeing him?"

"Greg?"

"That's the one. It's Saturday, I thought you might have a date tonight."

"No, Dad. We've known each other since school days, and really? He took me out for a birthday drink, but that's all it was. We're just friends."

Her father only nods, and Vera circles around the widow's walk, glancing at the sky over the water, then in the other direction at the sky over town. "I *have* been seeing someone, though. Derek. Derek Cooper."

Her father had been leaning his elbows on the railing, studying the sky intently. Now he turns his head to look at her. "From the hardware store?"

"You know him?"

"The one whose little girl died."

"Abby. Yes. We've been seeing each other a little bit. He did some work here on the house, and, well … it just sort of happened." She takes a long breath and turns up her sweater collar. "I really care about him. But then, I don't know. This is a hard time for him, around the holidays, especially since it's when his daughter died. I understand that. But Dad? I'm not sure if he's ready for a relationship. It seems like he's got a lot to deal with still, whether it's Christmastime or not."

"What do you mean?"

Vera stands beside her father, crosses her arms in front of her and looks out over the cove, so calm under the afternoon sky. "It's just that he'll be fine, and we'll have a nice time at dinner, or decorating, and then he gets really quiet and pulls back. It's so traumatic to have lost a child the way he did, and I know he's still grieving. I don't want to get in the way of that, to take away from whatever he needs to deal with."

"You? Get in the way?"

"It feels it, sometimes, mostly when he withdraws. It's like he doesn't want to share that part of his life with me."

Her father looks out at the sky and the wisps of white crossing it like streaks of paint. "Vera. Did you ever think that maybe it's something else? It could be that it's all new to him, having you in his life, and he's not sure *how* to share something so deeply personal with someone special."

"I don't know, Dad. It might be an issue he can't get past. Or maybe it's me who can't get past it."

She pulls a scarf up around her neck beneath the sweater and leans on the rail beside her father. They're quiet for a couple minutes.

"I think those clouds mean a change is coming," her father finally says. "Not right away, but they're an early sign."

"Of snow?"

He doesn't answer at first, and she waits, watching the sky until he speaks. Then she silently watches her father talk about what he loves most.

"Snowflakes are so beautiful. Their symmetry and delicateness is something to behold. Especially the perfect crystals. But you know, Vera. Most snowflakes are actually distorted or disproportionately shaped. So much happens to any single one as it moves through the clouds and deals with the different elements: humidity and wind and temperature." He stops then, watching those distant cirrus clouds for a long moment, then turns and looks directly at Vera. "Very, very few make it to the ground in perfect shape."

seventeen

LATER THAT AFTERNOON, VERA PUTTERS in her kitchen. She straightens and glues a loose tile on her backsplash, tightens a screw in one of the white-painted Windsor chairs, but keeps returning to the window, regardless. The view, across some of the yard and driveway, is of her big brown barn, nestled on a gently sloping hill. From this angle, she can't see the cove. But the far side of the barn, with its large double doors accented with crossbeams and wrought-iron handles, opens completely to the water view. Her thought is that at one time—maybe a century ago—ships came into the cove with deliveries of grains, or goods, and warehoused them in her barn. One thing's for certain: The planked, distressed walls belie all she's found stored inside it.

She'd gotten a lot of research done this past week and talked to a few more sources for her latest article, this one for the *Providence Post*. A freelance piece that could be significant. And she has to finish it up, but makes a quick decision before it's too late, one that has her put away her small toolbox and instead tuck her jeans into shearling-lined suede boots and throw on her red-plaid pea coat, before rushing out to the barn with a few large brown bags. It'll only take a minute; she knows exactly what she needs. Now if only Derek is where she hopes he'll be, her plan will work.

The drive through town is short, and she pulls into Cooper Hardware just after it closed for the day. But she's relieved to see Derek is still there, out back. He's crouched beside his boat in jeans and a warm cargo jacket and hat, with work gloves on, moving a power buffer over a wax compound he'd applied. His arm works methodically and carefully in a circular motion as he brings the boat's fiberglass to a pure shine.

"Derek," she calls out, hurrying over with her brown bags.

He stops the buffer and stands, holding it in his hands. "Hey, Vera."

She sees how intently he looks at her, as though trying to believe she's here. After leaving her behind at the tree-lighting ceremony, it's not surprising. That was reason enough to stay away. Instead she steps closer and reaches into one of the bags. "I hope you don't mind," she says, pulling out a couple model train cars. "But I was putting out this pretty train set in the barn. You know, for my holiday tag sale?"

He nods and sets the buffer down on the ground near the boat, then takes off his gloves.

"There's a nice spot for it. A shelf runs completely around the barn loft, so it's a good place to run a Christmas train, around and around. And you know, I set out some pine trees and little snow banks along the track. Well anyway, a couple cars don't seem to work and I was wondering if you could take a look at them?"

"Now?"

She shrugs and hands him the cars.

"What's the matter with them?"

"The locomotive won't move on the track." She points to one of the two red cars he holds. "And its horn doesn't work."

He turns the train car over and looks at the bottom, running his thumb over the silver wheels beneath it.

"And the caboose," she adds, pointing to the other car. "It doesn't light up. It's supposed to, isn't it?"

He studies the red-and-gold caboose with green garland painted along its edges. "Seems it," he says, looking up at Vera then and waiting.

She smiles quickly. "Well. I know you're busy and all. But I thought if you could stop by to try them on the track, maybe you could get them running for me?"

"You're sure they don't work? You tried the controls properly, plugged things in?"

She nods. "I can wait, while you polish the boat."

"You want to do this now?" He looks from the train cars to his boat. "All right. I can finish up here later."

"No! No, wait." She reaches into another brown bag and pulls out a long string of white twinkly lights. They hang tangled and bunched up from her hand. But she smiles hopefully while shaking them out and saying, "You finish waxing and I'll help, too. With your boat."

He looks at her lights. "Vera, I've got Christmas lights for it already."

"But I'll bet not this kind. Look." She walks to his boat and clips two ends of a three-strand swag of lights along the side rail, then turns to him with a raised eyebrow.

"Those are pretty fancy." He laughs. "Really, I only use a single strand of lights, Vera. Just to outline the shape."

"Yup, that's what I figured. Typical man thinking." She looks from him, to her swag of lights, then back at him. "So I brought enough to line both sides of your vessel. Because really," she says, her eyes tearing up as she drops her voice to a whisper, "these look like jewelry, like a sparkling necklace. And what little girl doesn't love jewelry?" She stands there holding another set of the lights, waiting for his answer. Which he doesn't give, she notices.

Not until he glances at his watch first, then rubs his knuckles along his jaw. "Okay," he relents.

"Perfect. So anyway, I'm just going to start hanging these on the sections you already waxed." And she does, lifting the next strand to the boat side. "Because Abby would *love* them."

When she hears him moving, she takes a peek and sees that he's put his work gloves back on and is picking up the buffer, glancing at her as he does, too, oh she doesn't miss that.

"I'm sorry about the other night, Vera. When I left you at the tree-lighting thing."

"That's okay."

"No, it really isn't. And I want you to know that even though it doesn't always seem it, I *have* made peace with Abby's death, I really have. It's just that this time of year is different. You know, it triggers stuff."

"Well, of course it would." Vera strings along her swag of twinkling lights, fussing with them to straighten each strand precisely. "So many special times must come back to you, when you think *Oh, I remember when*, or *Hey, Abby used to hang the tinsel this way,* or *That's a Christmas carol she loved.*" She shrugs while looking at her lights. "Things like that."

"You know," he says, buffing a small circle on the boat, then stopping. "I don't talk about Abby much because most people are uncomfortable with it." He looks at the boat and lifts the buffer again, circling it over a small section. "They don't really know what to say. But with you, it's different."

She smiles and nods as she clips on another swag. "So this boat must be the lead boat at the festival, right?"

"I thought I was done finalizing the procession, but I got a few more calls from interested boaters, so I've got to work them in. But my boat always leads the way. Always."

"I thought so. So the thing is, Derek, it has to be grand. You want it to really stand out as the most significant boat on the cove."

He polishes a section of the boat side, talking over the sound of the buffer. "I actually map out the procession ahead of time. Whoever's participating registers first and I set it up like a boat parade. Each vessel is lined up based on size, how its decorations fit with the theme, and even how it'll look visually on the cove once all the lights are turned on."

"Sounds like quite an operation."

He steps back and checks the section he buffed, lightly running his hand over it. "We start out on the water in the dark with very few lights. Just enough to see. And one by one, the boats light up. In order."

Vera sets down her next strand of lights and goes over to Derek, taking his buffer and setting it down, then taking his hand and giving a tug. "Come on," she insists. "Can you finish this tomorrow? Because I have something you really need to see."

"What do you think?" Vera steps aside as she opens the door onto her widow's walk. Derek follows behind and walks to the railing. "See that light reflecting on the water?" she asks. "The cove always catches the last bit of sunset like that." She looks at his face studying the water from this vantage point. "I'm glad there's still some light for you to see."

"This is amazing. It really looks different from up here."

"I know. That's why I wanted you to see it. And I was thinking, maybe you can map out your procession from here. You know, come back during the day when there's sunlight and visually plan the whole thing. I'd love to help. We can set a couple chairs out here and work it out?"

"I've got a photo album of the boats from other years. I can bring that too, so you'll have an idea of how the procession looks." He scans the water while he's talking. "We can work from that, adjusting the boat order for this year."

The sun sets further behind a line of trees cast in black silhouette now. Derek still looks out over the darkening water and Vera's not sure what exactly he's feeling, seeing the cove darken at dusk, this place where he lost his child. "Well, you let me know when you want to do this," she says, "and I'll get some of Brooke's apple muffins and put on fresh coffee and we'll plot out the whole Deck the Boats procession, okay?"

He doesn't say anything, and she's not sure if he'll go ahead with her plan until he finally turns to her. "Thank you, Vera." He takes her hand in his. "It means a lot." He looks back out over the water as though that's what has quieted him. "I used to hate this time of day," he says then. "There was something about the darkness that made me sad for Abby, thinking of the horrible darkness she faced. But being up here, it helps. There's light left in the sky, right at the horizon."

"There is. And when the sun goes completely down, the moon rises, and starlight lightens the water, too. So there's always light from up here," she whispers.

They look out together. "Abby would've loved this bird's-eye view," Derek says. "It feels like you're just soaring."

"And do you see those clouds?" The clouds her father pointed out earlier are dark streaks against the sunset sky. "There, out on the horizon? They're cirrus clouds."

He nods.

"My father says they mean change is coming. Snow, he hopes." She leans into Derek beside her, looping an arm through his. "The wonder of snowflakes, Derek, is their impermanence. Each one is a piece of art, nature's art. Delicate white shapes in so many pretty patterns, but the thing is? They're all fleeting. They don't stay. As soon as they land, they change. They melt, or their delicate edges go round, and in no time at all, they're gone. It's why we're so in awe of them when we see them gently falling." She closes her eyes for a moment and hopes he'll understand what she's saying. "What makes them so very, very special is the short time that something so precious is here with us."

❧

"How do you do it?" Derek asks quietly. In the twilight's stillness before she answers, he hears only the distant slow-lapping waves reaching the cove's shore.

"Do what?"

He turns to Vera on the widow's walk, the sky and water darkening into one. "Make it okay. No matter what I'm feeling, you just take it and, I don't know, give it your snowflake spin and suddenly what scares me, or breaks my heart, becomes something beautiful."

She smiles then, but doesn't say a word. Because this time, he knows, it's up to him. As daunting as it is to let himself love her, love someone, anyone again, he's the one who has to decide it. She brought him to this moment and steps back from it, he knows, to see what he'll do with it.

So when a breeze lifts off the evening water, he brushes a strand of hair from her cheek, his hand pressing it back behind her ear and staying there as he leans in and kisses her. Behind closed eyes, he feels her reach around his waist and hold him close. He kisses her longer then, both hands cradling her face, and the kiss grows so insistent, so deep, he finally has to stop, physically stop, pull back and rest his forehead to hers, only breathing. Because with Vera, there is no darkness, and the insistence is because he *wants* those light moments again. Craves them. Beyond the widow's walk, the midnight-blue horizon is edged with a smudge of lavender light from the setting sun. And still he's only breathing. Only hearing the gentle waves. Only touching her face.

"Vera. Beautiful Vera," he finally whispers. "Let's go inside."

Taking his hand, she leads him down the widow's walk stairs to her bedroom. With just a bedside lamp shining on a faded scrolled wallpaper she's yet to remove, Vera draws the curtains over the windows before shutting off that light, setting their coats over a chair and turning to him in the darkness. And when he lies with her on the bed, lying on his side facing her, he wonders if she knows. If she senses how many years have passed for him, when the night was only darkness, and nothing else.

But now, even though he can't see it, can't see the dark sky with tiny stars just emerging from behind those thin, wispy clouds, he knows it's there. Some things are always there and always will be there. Love, and loss too. Longing, and happiness. It's not just one or the other. There's *always* the other, shimmering on the edge of the horizon. Being so close to the cove, knowing the sky above it shines some small celestial light on its water, this moment with Vera gives him that.

Reaching for his face, her thumb strokes his skin, moving along his chin, his throat. The sensation of her touch, and her mouth, has him close his eyes remembering that moments can be beautiful. *Derek*, she whispers with her hand slipping off his shirt and reaching for his shoulder, pulling him close and saying soft words he hasn't heard for so long. Words that lighten the edge of the darkness and lead him to turn to her, to stroke her face, to draw his hands along her body. Each moment one he'd almost forgotten. When he moves over her, pressing her hair back, looking at her face, her neck, her eyes, kissing her tenderly, slowly, he hears her whisper again, hears her say his name.

But it is when her hands skim across his back with the softest touch, bringing a physical sensation to him, making him aware of each kiss, each sound, each second passing beneath the rising moon on this early winter night, the sky outside the same as it's always been, the water ever shifting beneath it … that is when love and possibility return to him as sure as some innate tide.

And he knows then, really knows, how because of only her, time finally moves forward again.

eighteen

"OH BY GOSH, BY GALOSHES!" Vera's father reports on the Monday morning weather segment. "This first storm of the season has the potential to be a record-breaker, folks."

"Please, no," Vera says. She stands stock-still in her fluffy bathrobe with a big mug of hot coffee cupped in her hands while staring at her little kitchen television set. Jingles sits on the windowsill, his raccoon tail hanging along the wall, as he watches brown leaves swirl in the wind outside.

"It's only Monday," her father continues, "so it's too soon to know the exact details. But we're definitely expecting a major storm arriving late this week. The approaching low-pressure system is drawing in cold air from Canada, which will keep this an all-snow event. And if what I'm seeing on the models continues, some areas could receive up to a foot of the white stuff!"

Vera glances out her kitchen window toward the sky, slams her coffee cup down on the counter such that it startles the cat, who jumps to the floor and runs under the table. "Oops, sorry Jingles, didn't mean to spook you." She gives him a quick pat before running upstairs to shower and change with a sneaking suspicion that her father's onto something. It was in his voice, an excitement he subdued until he can report for certain that this storm will be a doozy.

And if that's the case, she's got lots to do in the meantime.

Derek's been hearing it all morning now. Talking to hardware store customers is as good as watching the news; they all tell him a storm's coming and they want to pick out a tree before they're covered in a foot of snow. The store hasn't sold this many trees in one morning all season long. When his customers add snow shovels and a bag of ice melt to their orders, it's as good a prediction as he needs.

But as he finishes tying a netted balsam fir to a car rooftop, the last person he cares to talk to about the weather, at least for now, is the one in her red-plaid pea coat, earmuffs over her blonde hair, snowflake mittens on her hands, who just arrived and is studying the largest trees over on the other side of the lot.

Derek turns away, but he knows, oh he just knows that Vera is working her way over to him. "You're all set," he says with a light knock on the driver's side window of the car. "Merry Christmas to you."

"Will you be giving sleigh rides soon?" the man asks as he rolls down the window.

"This weekend. Carriage rides, unless that snow comes. Then we'll bring out the sleigh."

The man driving lightly toots the horn and slowly pulls out of the parking lot, leaving Derek wishing there was another customer's car behind his waiting for a tree. Instead, there's Vera.

"Hey, Derek," she says, smiling as she nears.

"Vera," he answers while taking off a leather glove. He shakes it out then carefully pulls it back on.

"How are you today?" she asks, stopping just shy of him.

"Okay. Was there something you needed?"

"Needed?" She looks closely at him.

"I'm busy."

"I'll bet. My dad says snow's on its way. Did you see his forecast?"

"I've actually been working all morning." He walks toward the trees and straightens some left leaning crooked by anxious customers.

"Derek?" Vera asks while following behind him.

He turns around quickly. "What is it?"

She stops with a short breath. "I just wanted to find a tree before the snow falls, that's all."

The wind gusts suddenly and he turns his collar up against it. "Take your pick."

She walks between two rows of large white pines, shaking her head. "The needles are too long on these. The ornaments might slip right off. And I need something taller."

He picks up a broken branch from the ground and tosses it to the side. "If you're going to be long, well, I've got things to do."

"Oh. I thought maybe you'd help, and we could decorate it this week?" She turns to another row of trees, tall balsam firs, and reaches her hand to a branch, touching the tip of it gently. "Derek?" She looks over at him when a young couple walks past, laughing while carrying a large tree to the netting area. "Is something wrong?" she asks after they're gone.

He straightens a tree leaning against the frame beside Vera. "I talked to Bob Hough earlier. He stopped by and bought a tree."

"The fire marshal?" she asks.

"You'd know that, wouldn't you?"

"Know what?"

"That he's the fire marshal. You'd know that after talking to him the other day. Because Bob's got a big white boat he decorates each December for Abby."

Vera walks to another tree, silently pulling it upright and checking how tall it is.

"He said you talked to him for a story you're writing for some Rhode Island paper. Something about a feature story on Addison's Christmas boat parade."

Vera looks a little longer at the tall fir, then sets it back against the wood frame.

"Excuse me," he hears as another couple approaches. Derek turns impatiently to them. "Do you have anything narrow?" the man asks. "Our tree has to go in a corner and can't be too wide."

"Over there," he tells them, pointing near the store. "The smaller trees are in that section. The Fraser firs might work for you." When he turns back to Vera while the couple is still thanking him, she is standing close, looking straight at him.

"Yes, okay?" she begins right away, huddled into her coat against the cold. "Yes, I am writing that piece. They're so excited to read it and there are even boaters interested in joining in. Or expanding Abby's tribute there, in Rhode Island."

135

"Why didn't you tell me?"

She turns up her hands. "I was going to. But I wanted to surprise you with it."

"Surprise?" He looks long at her. "What a nice coup for you."

"What?"

He begins walking alongside the trees, wanting to just keep walking. To not even bother with Vera, with Christmas. They'd never amount to anything, not anymore. So he turns quickly to face her and she nearly walks right into him, she'd been following so closely. "A nice coup, a way back into the big time. I don't really appreciate you cashing in on my grief, or on Abby's death."

"Is that how you see it, Derek? Cashing in?" She reaches out and takes his gloved hands in hers. "You don't understand. It's not about the money."

"Well, Vera. Why don't you enlighten me?"

An awkward moment passes before she explains. "Okay. For starters, my fee's actually being donated to Addison's Search and Rescue team. I wanted to do that, for you."

"And what else did you do?" he asks, stepping so close she has to take a step back. "Get me to your widow's walk Saturday night just to get your headline?" He pulls his hands away and turns toward the store, brushing past a family with two small children.

"How can you say that?" she calls after him, and so he stops. Just stops and looks up to the sky while she continues. "I wanted to share a touching Christmas story in the spirit of the season."

He turns again to face her. "So my daughter's death is a Christmas story now?" And he sees, out of the corner of his eye, the way the mother nearby puts a hand on each of her toddlers' shoulders to quickly steer them away and out to their car as the father looks back at him and Vera.

"No! No, Derek." Vera pushes a blowing strand of hair out of her face, and Derek supposes she's trying to put the right spin on one day that—not often, but sometimes still—taunts his emotions. And he gets the feeling she clearly knows that now. "Stop twisting up my words!" she insists. "Abby's story is about children, and people coming together." She steps closer, eyeing a couple watching them from the next row before sliding a mittened hand over a branch, testing it for dry needles. "And love, Derek," she says quiet enough for only him to hear. "It's about love. You can't think—"

"*Don't* tell me what I can and cannot think, Vera. It's not your place."

"Well I'm sorry," she answers, while her eyes tear up.

"So what is it, you're looking for a job in Rhode Island now? Addison's a layover between Boston and Providence, is that it? And what am I, a little entertainment for you?"

They both turn and look at Derek's father approaching when he calls out to them, pulling on a green jacket as he nears. Zeus trots along close behind him. "Hey! What's going on out here with you two?"

Derek looks at Vera and waits a second. It's a second when there's so much he can do; it's filled with choices. He can apologize to his father for carrying on too loudly in the tree lot, or he can take Vera's hand and walk her out to the back of the lot and talk this all out. And he wants to do it all, to make peace with both of them, but his anger at learning about Vera writing a story about his daughter, working on it without telling him, is even greater. Because it means there's a possibility of losing her now, too.

"She wants a tree," he tells his father. "Give her a hand, would you? So she can be on her way."

As he walks back toward the store, Derek hears her. Because still, he's listening for her voice, and he almost stops at the sound of it. "I'm very sorry, Mr. Cooper. I know you've got trees to sell here, and I'm not sure what just happened."

And Derek can guess that his father *does* know what happened because he's seen Derek's emotion plenty in the past five years. So without even turning, he figures his father gently takes Vera's arm to smooth things over. "Well, let's find you the right one," he says—loud enough for Derek to hear—no doubt shooting a glance back after he says it, annoyed with his son for walking away from this beautiful woman who means no harm. "It's got to be one that speaks to you."

❧

"Hold on to your hats, folks! This storm has a lot of potential, but the timing's still tricky." A multicolored map of the United States fills the TV screen behind Leo Sterling. With her dinner cooking on the stovetop, Vera watches her father's early evening forecast. "The areas in blue and purple indicate the greatest snowfall potential."

"Swell." She lifts a lid and stirs the pot of simmering green beans.

"Authorities are advising emergency precautions, regardless of the snowfall amounts. Because either way, it's shaping up to be a strong storm. You can check our website for the list of supplies you should have on hand. Things like fresh batteries and flashlights. Bottled water, too. You might want to stock up on firewood because power outages could leave you without heat. In which case—"

"Dress in layers," Vera says with him. "Layers and a hat, to keep in body warmth."

"I'll be keeping my eye to the clouds all week. Those clouds formed by millions of tiny water droplets. Droplets that, simply put, only have to freeze and become tiny snow crystals to get things going." The screen pans to photographs of last winter's snowstorms, of homes buried in snowdrifts, of icicles hanging like tinsel from rooftops. "Crystals that float through those clouds and keep growing, growing, until finally gravity tugs at them and down they fall, grounded in a blanket of white."

At the sound of a slow beeping outside, Vera looks out the window to see a Cooper Hardware Store delivery truck backing into her driveway. She quickly throws on her leather bomber, grabs the keys for the barn and rushes out the side door to meet it.

Well, gravity may ground snowflakes, but a good dose of reality is all it takes to ground Vera. Because one look at the senior Mr. Cooper and a part-time high school worker getting out of the truck to deliver her huge Christmas tree brings her right down to earth. Any vision, any hope of Derek stepping down out of that delivery truck in his cargo jacket and jeans, scarf and hat over dark brown hair, maybe holding a hot coffee, checking out the cove water, kissing her, standing beside her, helping her center the largest, tallest, biggest tree she could find in the barn double doorway so that she has a place to hang the remaining boxed ornaments, maybe staying for dinner— well, that vision is long gone and her heart grounded by the reality of his absence, but good.

nineteen

SOMETIMES VERA THINKS IT'S EASY to time travel while walking along the street that leads to her house at the cove. Usually it happens beneath the slant of late-afternoon sunlight, the low golden rays throwing long shadows. Strolling past olive-green and brick-red and dark-brown historic colonials with their paned windows, steep roofs, center brick chimneys, clapboard siding and white picket fences, she thinks she can just as easily be in the nineteenth century as the twenty-first. Why, a horse and buggy clip-clopping through the covered bridge on the other side of The Green and heading down the street wouldn't seem so out of place.

But today she doesn't have time for any of that easy daydreaming. Today, her father's latest words ring in her head. *Snow will fall at a rate of two inches an hour. Gale-force winds during the height of the storm can potentially bring visibility to near zero.*

With three days until Saturday, and until Derek's Deck the Boats Festival, and with the storm expected to hit over the weekend, there's still enough time. She hopes to convince her neighbors, each one of them, to bring Christmas back to their street in honor of the heart and soul of one little girl. A wreath, candles in the windows, lights on the picket fences—anything, anything at all to decorate this small street that serves as the entranceway to Addison Cove, to set the Christmas spirit for everyone who'll be driving by on their way to the Deck the Boats Festival—anything at all would be a touching tribute to Abby's life.

And so, walking up to each Cape Cod and saltbox and Georgian colonial doorway this Wednesday morning, ringing the doorbells of neighbors—some familiar, some not—Vera opens her own heart to them in her request. To decorate, once again.

Red felt cardinals with red glitter wings. Glass poinsettia ornaments. Sparkled snowmen and hand-stitched Santas. Clear glass balls filled with tiny green jingle bells. Frosted pinecones topped with striped ribbons. Glitter candy canes and miniature red mittens. Silver twig reindeer and gold beaded garland.

This is the last of it all. Every box has been pulled out of the barn's storage room, opened and emptied except for these remaining ornament cartons. For the past two days, Vera continued to carefully decorate her twelve-foot-tall Cooper Hardware Store Christmas tree. Now if Jingles would just stop batting off the ornaments from the lower branches, she could finish up here.

"Anybody home?" Brooke calls out while shouldering open the barn door with her arms chock-full of boxes. "Other than my favorite cat," she adds when a shining round ornament slides past her feet, Jingles in hot pursuit behind it.

"Back here!" Vera calls out from the other side of her towering tree. "Just follow the ornament trail."

"Ha. Jingles must be helping you decorate?"

"If you'd call it that," Vera says as she clips a felt cardinal to a lower branch for the cat to ponder. "Do you need help carrying stuff in?"

"The more the merrier. Because TGIF, I'm ready to jingle all the way into this weekend, and my trunk's overflowing with cakes for Deck the Boats."

They bring in all the boxes of pastries that Brooke fit in her car this trip. "It'll be so much easier to restock my tent at the festival tomorrow by having these right here," Brooke says. They carefully line boxes and boxes of Christmas coffee cakes on a long side counter, sorting them by flavor. "I've got one more carload to bring later."

"Wow," Vera says. "That's a lot of coffee cakes."

"Last year I had the only Pastry and Coffee tent, and sold out in no time. So I went a little overboard this year. I've got cherry-streusel, cranberry-nut, raspberry-chocolate chip. Heck, I even have a Christmas-tree-shaped coffee cake decorated with candied cherries for ornaments. Now what I really need is for Dad to get the snow to hold off till Sunday, and I'll be in good shape."

The barn windows rattle in a sudden gust of wind. "Gosh, I hope those tents hold up, too," Vera says. "That wind is really picking up."

"I know. We double staked everything and Brett's checking the other tents as we speak." Brooke pulls off her hat and mittens, slips out of her coat and walks over to the soaring, glimmering Christmas tree. "Would you look at this tree? It's magnificent!"

142

Vera follows her. "As soon as I'm done with the last of these boxes, I can schedule the tag sale. The whole Christmas Barn inventory is on display, top to bottom."

Brooke picks an embroidered snowman from the ornament box and considers where to place it. "How's Derek? He must be so busy getting the boats ready."

"I'm sure he is, but I wouldn't really know." Vera straightens the beaded gold garland as she walks the perimeter of the tree.

"Uh-oh. What happened?"

"We had a little falling-out, that's all."

"That's all?" Brooke picks up a glitter acorn and touches one tree branch before lifting another, looking for just the right spot. "I hope it's not serious?"

"I'm not really sure where we stand anymore. Haven't seen him in a few days now."

"Come on, Vee. Are you kidding? I thought things were good with you two."

"They were, until we didn't see eye to eye on something and, well, I'm not sure it'll work out."

"Huh." Brooke picks up one of the jingle-bell-filled glass balls and gives a little shake so that the cat comes running. He sits at her feet watching her jangle the ornament bells. "I better put this one up high. Don't need Jingles getting his paws on it." She finds a space after slowly walking around the tree. "Maybe Derek's just busy," she finally says, lifting a soft, round, cat-toy-sized ornament from the tree and rolling that one across the floor for Jingles to bat. "This Deck the Boats is a big thing around here."

"I don't know, Brooke. I was actually writing a profile of the festival for that Providence paper your mother-in-law sent me to. Derek found out and didn't like it."

"Why not?"

"I'm not sure. What he does with the boat festival just warms your heart, especially the way so many people come together for it. I really wanted to share that part of Abby's story. Her memory deserves to be honored, and celebrated, by more than just one town. Imagine the good it could do! Seems he thought I was just commercializing it."

"Ouch. A sensitive subject, but when I think about it, he probably overreacted. You know what it is?" Brooke asks. "He must be mad because he thinks you're leaving. On your way up and out of Addison. Because seriously, Vee? He tells *everybody* about the Deck the Boats Festival, so he's got no issues sharing and spreading the word."

"Whatever it is, we really argued and it wasn't good."

"Well everybody has a tiff now and then. But still. You should talk to him about it. I was so happy that you two found each other, I'm sure you can work it out. You had good intentions, he *has* to know that."

"I'd love to explain, but I couldn't get through to him the other day. He wouldn't listen."

"Maybe because he's under so much pressure right now. If you could've *seen* the turnout last year, you'd understand. There was no space left to park so people left their cars on your street and walked down to the cove. And it keeps getting bigger every year."

Vera wishes it were only that. That Derek was simply distracted and feeling stressed by the whole thing: the festival, the holidays, the busy hardware store.

"I mean," Brooke is saying as she walks toward the tree with a glitter reindeer in her hand, "people come from everywhere to see these decorated boats. It's amazing, because the first year, it was just Derek on his one boat with a lit Christmas tree, all by himself. Floating in the middle of the cove at night. And some people saw it, you know?" She hooks the deer on a branch, then lifts it off and looks for another spot. "And the next year, there were maybe four boats. And the next, well, it just got so big."

Vera opens the box marked *Tree Topper* while Brooke keeps explaining. She knows her sister is trying to distract her, to make her feel better, to convince her that Derek will come around, he's just busy. Because that's what sisters do; so she's quiet while Brooke does her sister thing.

"And then we started serving pastries. And another tent sells Addison sweatshirts. And hot chocolate. And what happens is that afterward, all the money raised goes to the Children's Hospital in Abby's name. And now carolers come, too, singing during the procession. And, well. You'll see." She hangs a snowman and turns to Vera. "You'll see."

Vera pulls out the tree topper, and would it be anything else but a large six-sided silver sparkle snowflake? "I guess our bigger concern right now is that Dad gets Mother Nature to hold off on that snow until Sunday," she says, holding the topper up for Brooke to see. "So the Deck the Boats Festival can go on as planned. For everyone's sake."

"No kidding," Brooke says with a worried glance over at her supply of festival coffee cakes. "That topper is all the snow I need to see before then."

twenty

GET OUT YOUR SHOVELS, AND put away the rakes. Because that's what you'll be needing, folks, from the looks of these snowflakes."

Vera pulls a coffee mug from her cabinet and pours a fresh cup, turning to watch her father in all his snow glory, sporting a snowflake-patterned wool cap this time as he unveils snow statistics to accompany this season's first storm.

"Billions of snowflakes can fall during a single storm, and from the looks of these clouds," the camera pans out to the ominous sky behind him, "we might not be able to keep up with the snowflake numbers. If I were a ship captain of yore, I'd cancel my voyage for this one."

Her father has taken the station's cameraman up to the widow's walk to give his Saturday morning forecast from that vantage point, and oh boy, the dramatic cove view will not disappoint his viewers. As chief meteorologist, he's definitely one-upping the competition with his exclusive on-site report.

Gray clouds hang low over the cove's dark water. Piles

of them, pressing on top of each other, getting more threatening each time Vera looks out. All she thinks is that they are so huge, and so heavy-looking, they must be weighed down with an incredible amount of snow that is about to bust out and blanket Addison.

"Three miles per hour. That's the average speed that a snowflake falls to the ground. And I'm sorry to report, that's the average speed we'll be driving once this storm hits. It's a doozy, folks."

Vera stands still, holding her steaming coffee cup close, sipping it and listening to her father talk about the largest snowflake ever documented, a flake nearly fifteen inches in diameter. If she could only make a wish on that documented winter star, just one wish bestowed on the grandest snowflake of them all, it would be this and only this: Please. Please hold off on dropping *any* snowflakes on Addison—one fifteen-inch flake or millions of tiny ones—just for one day, just for one man who needs this wish the most.

"Many of you are emailing the station asking if the Deck the Boats Festival is still on. As of now, yes it is, but stay tuned for updates because the latest models call for significant accumulations, with the potential for a foot or more. It's the timeline of this storm that is still uncertain. Light snow will overspread the state late morning. But some models show the storm stalling, so conditions *may* not deteriorate until late tonight and into early tomorrow."

Yes, Vera thinks, *her wish has been heard!* She crosses her fingers on both hands and glances out the window hoping Derek can get his boat in the water, then looks back to the television set and her father, who is actually standing two floors above her on her widow's walk, trying to decipher the skies.

147

"Other models show heavy snow by dinnertime. Regardless, it's coming, and once the storm hits full-force, all that snow combined with gusting winds will produce whiteout conditions. Which will have you waking tomorrow to a magnificent winter wonderland."

The camera pans out to those bulging clouds over the sky, bulging with those billions of flakes.

It's the sound that worries Vera. By early afternoon, she notices it. It's almost a hiss, the soft yet insistent noise that comes seemingly from her windows. Her single-paned, inefficient windows that do little to keep out the cold, and apparently little to keep out sound, too. Because she's hearing a soft, fluctuating hiss that is foreboding.

Diamond dust, she thinks. They're the smallest snowflakes of all, so small the human eye can't usually see them. And she knows what can produce them. Storms. Epic snowstorms. But mostly at high altitudes. If diamond dust ever makes it to the ground, well, this must be what it sounds like.

What is most frightening is that when she goes to the window, any window, whether the kitchen window where Jingles takes up the entire sill—and then some—looking out at the barn, or the living room window opposite her brick fireplace, or the dining room windows on her newly painted gold walls, it's always the same. The noise is there, but when she looks out, she doesn't see anything. That's how tiny the snowflakes hitting the windows are; it doesn't matter if they're branched crystals or sectored plates or split-stars or needles or diamond dust, they're invisible to her eye. And she remembers her father's rule of thumb: The smaller the flakes, the bigger the storm.

But never was there a time when the flakes were so darn tiny she couldn't even see them. It scares her enough to hurry to the hall closet for her coat, and wouldn't you know it? The doorknob comes right off in her hand as she tugs the sticking door open. She quickly tosses the knob on the closet floor and puts on her jacket, scarf, hat, mittens and shearling-lined boots to hike herself right down to the cove and check on her sister.

Every minute now brings a new urgency. She locks the front door of her old Dutch colonial, runs down the steps and across her yard to the street. A motion catches her eye before she even reaches the cove: The food and craft tent walls blow and billow in the wind as though they are taking great gasping breaths.

"Brooke?" Vera yells, shielding her eyes from those invisible flakes feeling like tiny needles on her skin. "Brooke!" she yells again as she slaps at the canvas wall of her sister's portable tent, her voice lost in the wind.

Brooke unzips a side wall. "Vera!" She grabs her by the arm and tugs her inside. "Brrr. Come in, quick, so I can zip this up."

Vera sees a small table set up with Brooke's coffee cakes, some sliced and wrapped, others whole cakes in boxes. "I can't believe the festival isn't cancelled."

"I know, I hear those darn snow crystals hitting the tent now. At least nothing's sticking on the ground yet." Brooke straightens a plate of coffee cake slices on the table. "Maybe they can get the boats in early?"

"A few are lined up out there on trailers, waiting to launch. It's crazy, though. The storm's coming!" As Vera says it, a gust of wind tugs at the tent walls.

"Is Derek out there?" Brooke asks. "Maybe you can

149

talk to him and convince him to postpone."

"His boat's first in line to go in the water. But I don't see his truck, he must have dropped the trailer and left."

Brooke pulls open the tent zipper a few inches and peeks out. "Do you believe there are already cars parked, reserving their spot so they have a good view of the procession?"

"No way."

"I'm telling you, Vera. The whole town comes out for this." She looks out again, then back at Vera. "Well. They come for Derek."

Vera shakes her head. "Listen. I'm going back home to try to get in touch with him. But I don't want you driving later in the storm. You'll stay overnight at my house when you're done here."

"What about Mom?"

"Mom?"

"Dad's dropping her off here on his way in for the afternoon shift."

"You're kidding." Vera checks her watch. "I'll try to reach her, too."

"Okay. And hey, take my keys," she says as she pulls her purse off a shelf. "My car's behind the tent. Just drive it to your place, okay? So it'll be safe in your driveway during the storm."

Vera takes her keys and heads out, amazed at the cars that have since pulled into the cove parking lot. Once home, she first goes up to the widow's walk to see the conditions from there. And still, *still* she feels the tiniest of crystals hitting her face, though she can't really see them.

And what scares her even more is the idea of *all* the things she cannot see—grocery store parking lots crazy with last-minute shoppers; Cooper Hardware selling out of shovels, maybe trying to cover up their remaining Christmas trees; the town sand trucks loading their beds; authorities issuing a snow-parking ban; the untold volumes of snow weighing down the gray clouds; and Derek, Derek somewhere, in his cargo coat, sweater and jeans, snow boots and gloves, checking in with the weather service, or deliberating the festival options with Bob Hough, not answering her call on his cell, panicked on this one day when he reaches out to his Abby.

Suddenly, as she worries about all she cannot see, there's a change. The flakes feel softer on her skin, so she pulls the mini-magnifier from her jacket pocket first. Then she extends her arm in the air, straight out over the widow's walk railing, giving the snowflakes the perfect landing place. When she holds her magnifier to her arm, it finally happens. They're visible, the first of tiny crystals, glimmering winter stars. What worries her even more, though, is the way her entire sleeve covers with flakes in a matter of moments until there are so many, they are indistinguishable from one another and form a blanket of white. Just like that. Frighteningly fast.

Derek drops the plow on his pickup truck and pushes through the snow in the cove parking lot, a white plume of powder flying off the plow. If he can just keep a path cleared to the water, they can get the boats in. It doesn't really matter how many people arrive to see the decorated boats. It doesn't even matter if *all* the trailered boats make it into the water. All that really matters is his. His boat with the Christmas tree mounted in the bow, this time with colored twinkling lights. For the first time. His boat with Vera's swags of jeweled lights along the sides, looking like an elegant boat necklace. He's sorry now for the words he said outside the hardware store. If it weren't snowing this hard, he'd have had a few minutes to stop at her house when he'd driven past. Lamplight was shining in her windows, a large balsam wreath hung on her door and the two small fir trees outside her barn were illuminated with twinkling lights. Some part of him was glad for that, knowing that she was home, safe and sound, in this monster storm descending upon them.

A small crowd of people gather toward the back of the cove parking lot, huddled in the blowing snow and clutching thermoses of hot chocolate and coffee. They don't see his worry, his panic to get that boat in the water for Abby, to light up her Christmas tree. They never heard his words to her when he held her lifeless body in his arms, feeling the weight of her waterlogged clothes, touching her damp face. They didn't know he'd promised to love her always and that she shouldn't be afraid, that he'd always be with her somehow. They didn't know that the only way he could figure to be with her was here, on the water. Because what child should be alone at Christmastime?

Now if he can just keep the pathway to the water cleared. His truck plow pushes through another swath of snow that is coming down faster than he can keep up with. If it weren't for headlights on the far side of the lot, he could hardly make out Bob Hough's truck over there, plowing too. Between the both of them, they might be able to get a couple of boats out on the cove. But as long as he gets at least *his* boat idling out there for a little while, with its tree lit up, that'll be enough. Abby will be remembered.

After plowing the path from his trailered boat to the boat ramp, the windshield wipers brushing rapidly across the windshield, the defroster blowing fully, he puts his pickup into reverse and starts to back up so that he can give the path one more go-through. But he's forced to stop when a red-plaid pea coat appears in the distance in the rearview mirror. A red-plaid coat with white snowflake mittens, over jeans tucked into lace-up snow boots with a fur cuff, headed cautiously, but directly, toward his truck. He rolls down the window when she nears.

"Derek!" she calls out, her voice cutting through the wind, her eyes squinting against the blowing snowflakes.

"Vera, what are you doing out here?"

"That's what I came to ask you," she answers, breathless in the cold. She stands close beside his truck. "Derek," she says, a sad smile pausing her words. "I'm sorry about the other day, and I want to talk to you. But first, well, I think you should cancel the festival."

"What?"

"It's too dangerous. The way that wind's blowing over the water, it's so rough out there. And the currents are strong. Please, Derek, please don't do this."

"Vera, you don't understand. I have to. And we've got things cleared, Bob and I. We'll be all right."

A strong gust of wind blows, making Vera turn away from it, from the stinging bite of its cold on her skin, from its force whipping her hair. When she turns back, she's either crying or the wind brings tears to her eyes. "Derek, it's not safe." She holds her mittened hands to her face to block the blowing snow. "You could be hurt out there, or need help, and no one could get to you," she says, huddled into her scarf and coat, her words nearly lost in the noise of the storm, of Bob's truck plow, of the waves rising.

"I'll be okay, Vera. I know what I'm doing." He glances through the windshield at the snow piling up again in the parking lot. "I just can't really talk now."

Vera backs up a step. "But what about the others? You can't risk losing another life on the water. Please, at least postpone."

"Don't you get it? Today's the day. This is the day Abby died. Even if I go out there alone, I have to do this, for her."

"But can't you find another way? These people need to be home before the roads are impassable. If you give the word, they'll leave, Derek. They'll listen to you. It'll be quiet, then. We can, I don't know, you and I can light up the widow's walk. We'll do something else to commemorate Abby."

He just looks at her, then looks in his rearview mirror only to see a line of cars pulling into the parking lot. "It's too late," he yells out to Vera over a gust of wind. "They want to see it, they want to be a part of it."

Vera looks over her shoulder at the traffic. He wonders if she understands that nothing will stop all of Addison from showing up. There's something about this night, this festival, that brings them all together. Maybe it's because they couldn't come together one day five years ago, and they pay their respects now by meeting up once a year, right here. No matter what.

She turns back to Derek. Tears streak her cheeks, her eyes squint against the icy snow. "Please don't do this," she whispers against the wind while stepping closer. Her mittened hands, mittens caked with snow, grip the edge of his open window. If he's not mistaken, what he sees in her face, too, is a new insistence. And with her next words—words that can't come easy, words he doubts she'd have said except for the danger he's facing—well, he knows exactly why there's an urgency now. The thing is, they're words he *never* saw coming, and they work, those words. They stop him. "I love you, Derek," she says, her head tipped.

He looks at her long enough through the biting snow for her to whisper, *Come back with me*. Long enough for the thought of cancelling Deck the Boats to become a possibility. How easy it would be to tell her to get in the truck and then head back to her house. It'll be warm inside, they'll light the fireplace, they'll talk this out.

He shoves his coat sleeve up and checks his watch, then looks out to Vera, shaking his head. "I'm sorry, Vera. Really, it's best if you head back where you'll be safe." He puts the truck in gear and hitches his head in the direction of her house, a huge home that is now just a looming faint shadow behind the thick snowfall.

She starts to say something, then whips around, her arms crossed in front of her against the cold and wind, and walks away. He watches her go, watches her pass the food and coffee tents battened down, pass the craft and sweatshirt tents zipped up tight against the gale-force wind, watches her glance back once, only once, before picking up her pace, first to a slow trot through the deep snow, and finally to a full-out run, slipping as she nears her house.

And when he loses sight of her in the late-afternoon darkness and the descending storm, he turns toward the water, drops his plow and pushes his truck through the encroaching snowdrifts, the engine straining with the effort.

twenty-one

WHEN VERA CAN'T EVEN SEE her house in front of her, she knows the whiteout conditions have arrived. The tall maples and oaks along her street bow their limbs to the wind and her boots sink deep into powdered snow, making walking treacherous. As she leaves the cove parking lot, something *does* catch her eye through the turmoil of the swirling storm. The entire street she lives on is aglow; all the old colonial houses on either side are lit up with twinkling wreaths on their doors, candles in windows, a few illuminated waving snowmen, and decorated picket fences. It looks like a Christmas gateway to the cove, and for her neighbors, she is so thankful. At least Derek has that much now.

And seeing all those pretty lights leading to the water, an idea comes to her, one that has her climb her front steps and run into the house to grab her keys to the barn. Jingles follows along behind her snowy boots, batting at a small clump of snow as she snatches the keys from the kitchen countertop and heads out back through the side door, sliding down the snow-covered steps to the long driveway leading to her barn. The twinkling lights on the small fir tree standing beside it light the way in the stormy evening.

But she stops when a noise carries on the wind: a long, plaintive cry. It has her spin around and look back toward her house, peering through the falling snow. When the noise comes again, her eyes barely pick out Jingles sitting on the top step of the side stoop. She rushes back, sinking so deep the powder-soft snow reaches the top of her boots, scoops up her big raccoon cat and tucks her coat around him as she treks to the barn, bent over against the wind.

Once safe inside, she takes a deep breath, turns on a lamp that casts a golden light on the space and heads straight for the cross-beamed double doors facing the cove, Jingles following close behind. First she lifts the heavy latch, and with all the muscle she can muster, slides the wooden doors open against the snow. The winter storm rages on the other side of them, and still she's mystified by so many car headlights filling the cove parking lot, waiting for the Christmas festival. The townsfolk are as insistent on being there as Derek is, honoring his child.

Well, there's no way those decorated boats are going in the water this stormy night, not if she has anything to do with it. And so she turns back and considers her twelve-foot-tall fully decorated Christmas tree dripping with sparkling ornaments and garlands, rising in the open double doorway of her barn. Her dark tree. After another glance out to the cove, she reaches to the side wall and throws on the light switch.

If she's not mistaken, the change is instant as thousands of twinkling lights come on, unfurling their resplendent glow through the storm's blowing snow to the cove. And the night stills, somehow. The trucks plowing, the cars sliding through the parking lot, squeezing in and looking for a space amidst snowdrifts and boat trailers, all of them, every vehicle comes to a stop. As sure as snowflakes—and there's *no* missing those tonight—every pair of eyes has turned to her magnificent Christmas barn rising through the dark storm.

With no time to waste, Vera works her way through the barn to plug in every display, every mechanical caroler, every decorated tree, every Christmas village—including Brooke's extravagant miniature town crowded with pine trees and storefronts and bakery after bakery—every swag of green garland draped along shelves and banisters, every candle in each barn window, every snowman and reindeer, everything, until she arrives at the sparkling swan carousel, saving that one for last.

Before she can look outside again, she grabs her cell phone from her purse and calls Brooke, knowing she's out there in her tent with their mother in the midst of a raging snowstorm.

"Brooke!" she says when her sister answers.

"Vera? Holy cow, your barn, what a sight it is!"

"Never mind that for now. Listen, Brooke. I want you and Mom to leave, right away. Just close up your tent and get out of there. The snow's really coming down and it's dangerous to be out in it."

"I had the same thought. We're about to pack it up."

"Wait! Because what I want you to do is this. Direct everyone up here to the barn. Everyone! It's warm and safe inside and there's plenty of room for people to wait this thing out."

"Are you sure?" Brooke shouts into her phone over

the sound of the whistling wind.

"Absolutely. Get as many of those people here as you can. Hurry!"

By the time Vera gets to the double doors again and looks out, Brooke's husband, Brett, is standing in the cove parking lot, a flashlight in each swinging hand directing traffic toward her home. And ahead of him, Bob Hough is plowing a clear path through the snowdrifts straight from the cove to her driveway.

Before long, Vera turns to see Brooke and her mother walking into the barn, their coats and hats covered in white snowflakes, faces rosy red, their arms filled with boxes of coffee cakes from the tent. "That was fast," Vera tells them as she takes some of the pastries and sets them out on a counter.

"We got a ride from Bob." Her mother glances out the door behind her. "And get ready, Vee. The whole town's on its way."

Vera looks past them and sees a couple of her neighbors using their snowplows to clear the walkway from the house to the barn, while her long driveway is being cleared by Bob. But the best part? A line of headlights slowly snakes its way out of the cove parking lot, driving up the street, and if she's not mistaken, heading straight to her barn.

twenty-two

IT DOESN'T TAKE LONG. EVERYBODY was ready to seek shelter, Vera can see that now. Her barn double doors are still open to the cove, the massive Christmas tree casting its glittering light on the swirling snow outside. That view—the image of endless white snowflakes spinning against a midnight-blue sky, side-lit by the glow of her tree—becomes almost celestial.

But inside, the Christmas Barn has taken on its own magical glow. Vera stands up on the loft watching the families crowd in. *Ooohs* and *aaahs* rise to her as they set their gaze on the miniature villages and snowmen and reindeer and sleighs and the hundreds of glittering snowflakes hanging from the ceiling beams. Her brightly lit Christmas train that Derek fixed up chugs around and around the loft through valleys and hills of snow and pine trees, and the candy-cane alley is like a Christmas funhouse for the young children.

The group of carolers from the cove stands just outside the barn, bundled in scarves and hats and mittens, greeting those arriving with happy Christmas songs while the snow flies all around them. People inside pull off their damp hats and stamp their snowy boots on the wooden floor, looking around in sheer Christmas awe. Even Jingles is in awe, quietly perched on a loft railing near her, gazing down at the vast number of people below shedding their coats and gloves in the warm barn.

Quickly, Vera runs down the steps and takes a look out the side double doors to get a clear view of the cove parking lot. The last of the cars have left there, and so she returns to the loft. When Jingles bats a loose bell across the loft floor, the ringing gives Vera an idea. "Thanks, Jingles," she whispers as she picks up a red leather strap lined with six silver sleigh bells.

Standing at the loft railing, she looks out at the hundreds of faces below and raises the sleigh bells, jingling them loud enough for heads to turn toward her. "Can I have your attention please?"

With a couple more jangles of the silver bells, the crowd quiets and waits for Vera to continue as they huddle together, excited to be in her festive barn on this snowy night. When even the carolers step inside and close the red front entrance door of the barn, she clears her throat and begins. "Welcome, all! I am so glad you made your way here through the snow and hope everyone is safe and sound. Please make yourselves comfortable, feel free to browse the displays and decorations while you warm up a little."

A few people in the crowd wave quietly at her: friends she knows, neighbors. But other than that, everyone still waits, watching her. "I see some familiar faces, but for the rest of you who don't know me, I'm Vera Sterling." She tucks her hair behind her ear, unsure of how to handle the crowd. "Well, you probably know my dad, Leo Sterling.

He's the local weatherman, loving all this snow, I'm sure." She smiles nervously, then goes on in the silence. "So anyway, I bought this property a few months ago, and in the middle of fixing it up, came across a true hidden treasure—all the remaining inventory from the old Christmas Barn." She looks around the entire barn, from the snowflakes hanging from ceiling beams to a nutcracker shelf in the back. "I'm planning on having a holiday tag sale soon, so while you wait out the storm, have a look around at the beautiful Christmas history before you. And, in the meantime, well I'm just glad there's enough room here to celebrate this special night together."

A motion catches her eye then, at the still-open double doors off to the side. She turns to see Derek walking in, pulling off his hat and giving it a shake before eyeing the barn warmly lit up on such a dark night. This all happened so spur-of-the-moment, she'd never considered what he might think of it, or if he'd even show up. He gradually turns his gaze toward her in the loft right as Brooke hurries over to him with a large, hot coffee. It's precisely at that moment, when he takes the coffee from her and cups it close for warmth, that Vera gets another idea.

She steps back toward the center of the railing and gives the sleigh bells another jangle. "So anyway, with my dad being the chief meteorologist down at the station, I've got the inside scoop on this snowy weather. And I want each and every one of you to stay put until I get the green light from him." She clears her throat again while tucking her hair back behind an ear. "The good news is that with this storm blowing outside, I'm happy to share that we have a treat for you inside. My sister, Brooke, is serving up her famous Christmas-tree coffee cake tonight." She finds Brooke down in the sea of faces and her sister gives her a thumbs-up as she hurries over to the long counter near the door to set out napkins. She'd brought over enough coffee cake yesterday to feed an army, so this can definitely work. "If I'm not mistaken, there's candy-cane coffee cake, too, which is her specialty raspberry-cream-cheese concoction, and she's also brought cranberry-streusel coffee cake."

When another bell jingles from below, Vera searches the crowd to see her mother standing beside Brooke. A bell is in one raised hand while her other hand points to the large coffeepot, bringing sudden tears to Vera's eyes as her mom helps save the night.

"My mom will be pouring fresh hot coffee to go with Brooke's delicious pastries, and so ..." Vera hesitates. The howling wind draws her eye to the double doors and storm swirling outside, the snowflakes illuminated by the glow of her towering Christmas tree. "So," she continues as everyone watches her closely, waiting, "I guess we've got snowflakes and coffee cakes for all!"

The applause starts slowly and builds until everyone is clapping and talking and laughing at the thought of being stranded together inside her barn, with enough good food and good cheer to go around, and then some.

Vera jangles the sleigh bells one more time until the barn quiets. "And still, I want to remind you why we're here, after all. Even though the guys were not able to get the boats in the water in honor of Abby Cooper, my hope is this: That the light of this magnificent tree, decorated with old ornaments from all our pasts, reaches your hearts in the same special way."

In the hush of the barn, Vera seeks out Derek. When she sees him, and sees that he's watching her still from beside the double doors, as though he's keeping an eye on the cove too, she continues, a little quieter, a little less festive. "My hope is also that the tree's light shines far, far beyond, out to the cove, as well."

There really isn't another word she can say without choking up, her eyes already welling as she sees that Derek never stops watching her from below.

It is the small miracle of the carolers that saves her then. A miracle that starts with one soft, clear voice, one that has her turn to it, the beauty of its tone in the barn matched only by the solemnity of the moment.

Silent night, holy night ...

Other voices join in, one at a time at first, as though unsure.

All is calm, all is bright ...

Still more join in until a heartwarming chorus of so many voices rises past her solitary Christmas tree, to the swirling skies outside the big barn doors, beautiful and sad voices filled with love's pure light, delivering on the stormiest of nights—somehow, together, for one little girl, in a way that only small-town Addison could do— the sweetest heavenly peace.

twenty-three

At THE FIRST CHANCE, VERA stabs a hunk of raspberry-cream-cheese coffee cake and lifts it to her mouth. Her coat from last night still hangs over the back of one of the white wooden chairs in her kitchen, because that's the kind of unexpectedly wonderful night it was: No one wanted it to end. Standing at her table beneath the pendant lights, there's time enough to spear another slab of the sweet cake during the morning's brief lull, before it begins again. When the phone rings, she rolls her eyes up to the beadboard ceiling, stomps her foot, and walks to the phone while chewing a mouthful of cake.

"I'll get it," Brooke says as she rushes into the room and grabs the cordless.

Vera knows exactly what the call will be about. It'll be just like the nine other calls that came in since early this morning from people wondering when her holiday tag sale will happen. Calls from complete strangers, people she'd never met who were either at her barn last night or heard about the simply magical evening from friends and neighbors who were gathered there, celebrating

Christmas and snow and life together. She returns to the table in her dark emerald corduroys and thick turtleneck sweater, snowflake slippers on her feet and, this time more leisurely with Brooke handling the phone, has another piece of cake while the coffee percolates. When Brooke repeats their now well-versed line, saying, "Check the *Addison Weekly*, an announcement will be posted there soon," she knows she is right.

Everyone wants a nostalgic ornament from the old barn, a bit of history, a memory. Or they want a local hand-painted piece—a chapel, the wedding shop, a nursery greenhouse—to add to their own snow villages. Or they want that pinecone wreath, or the decorative sleigh with real velvet seats, or the manger scene. Something. They want anything, actually, and from the wistful sound of their voices, Vera thinks it has more to do with happiness at being a part of this special town than anything else.

Yes, everyone wants to be at the old Christmas Barn once again, even for a tag sale.

Brooke hangs up the phone and pours two big snowflake mugs of piping-hot coffee, setting them down as she sits at the table across from Vera.

"Did you talk to Mom today?" Vera asks.

"I did. They made it home okay last night and Dad's already at work now. I'm sure he was up at the crack of dawn celebrating the first snow, even though he had to clear it all from the driveway. Any snow is good snow, even driveway snow."

"I bet he'll make a first-snow snowman when he gets home, too." Vera looks out the window. The sky is lighter this morning, though snow still falls. Big, lazy stellar dendrites. Snow stars looping and drifting down from the clouds, leaving the perfect soft finishing touch on the foot and a half already on the ground.

"What an awesome night it was," Brooke says, sipping her coffee and slicing a piece of a Christmas-tree coffee cake for herself, her finger scooping up a candied cherry.

"I've never seen anything like it."

"I told you," Brooke says around a mouthful of cake. "Derek's Deck the Boats Festival really does something to people around here."

As if on cue, the phone rings again and Vera answers it. "Yes, thank you," she says. "I'm not sure yet when the tag sale will be. Yes, everything will be for sale." She pauses, then goes on. "Keep an eye on the paper, I'll be announcing the date soon."

When she hangs up, Brooke is packing last night's leftover coffee cakes. Her serving utensils soak in soapy water in Vera's kitchen sink. "Brooke," Vera begins. Her sister looks up from her packing, waiting. "I was thinking. Why don't you leave those things here?"

A slow smile breaks out on Brooke's face as she sets down a wrapped coffee cake and sinks back into her seat. She loops a burgundy scarf beneath her chin, pushes up her thick sweater sleeves and after a second, asks, "Are you thinking what I think you're thinking?"

Vera only nods.

"You're serious?"

She nods again. "Is it crazy? Or genius?"

"Genius or crazy, forget the tag sale, Vee. I mean, there's a full-blown Christmas shop out in that old barn. Seriously. You can go into business." As she says it, Jingles saunters into the kitchen and jumps up onto the window ledge, watching the big snowflakes float down, gently twisting and turning.

"My thoughts exactly. And remember this?" Vera opens a kitchen drawer and pulls out the yellowed piece of paper. She scoots a chair over right beside her sister, pushes the coffee cake dishes aside and presses open the paper on the table. "It's that letter we read, the one I found with the ornaments. From Alice. She used to run the Christmas Barn?"

Brooke glances at the handwritten note, then looks up at Vera. "It's a little bit sad, like she was missing the shop before she even left. I get that, but what are you saying?"

"Well, see the part about new beginnings?"

"Where she kind of gives her blessing on opening a Christmas shop again with the old inventory?"

"Right. And in my heart," Vera says while looking at the old letter, "I believe that's what she hoped for."

"That the Christmas Barn would reopen? You mean, like a full-time business?"

Vera shrugs. "It could work, don't you think?"

Brooke takes her mug to the counter and tops it off with hot coffee, then turns to Vera with a grin on her face. "Do *you* think so?"

"I might. Wait." Vera runs into her small office off the kitchen and returns with her leather planner. "Let me write some of this down."

"Okay, here's the journalist in you kicking in, Vee."

"Because it helps to see it this way. Now listen. When Alice ran the Christmas Barn, it was such an old gem, and really loved. It's been neglected for a few years, but it's sort of a diamond in the rough. If we can polish up the barn, and the business, I *do* believe we could make it work."

"We?" Brooke asks, cutting a thick slice of cranberry-streusel coffee cake this time.

"Come on," Vera persists. "Remember when you started working for Tom to help pay for culinary school?"

"Sure, part-time while I was taking the cooking classes."

"Yup. And the next thing I knew, you took over for the secretary when she went on maternity leave. And *then* you swapped out culinary courses for paralegal."

"Well it was a sure thing, working there. Cooking wasn't. And the money's good."

"Listen, Brooke. I know it's a good job, but is it your true calling? I'll never forget when you told me it's just so much more practical."

"It is, though. That's the way I am, practical. Unlike you, partly unemployed and living in this, okay, beautiful-but-needs-work house."

Vera raises her eyebrows at her sister. "And loving it, I might add. And wouldn't you *love* baking up a storm? A snowstorm of coffee cakes, right here?"

Brooke sets her fork down. "Wait. What exactly are you talking about? It's a Christmas shop."

"Was." Vera jumps up and runs to her kitchen side door, opening it wide so they can see the view straight out to the barn as they plan. "*Was* a Christmas shop. But Snowflakes and Coffee Cakes is part bakery, too."

"Snowflakes and Coffee Cakes?" Brooke laughs easily. "Oh, I can just picture it!"

"I'm serious, Brooke. Snowflakes and Coffee Cakes. It's the newly named Christmas Barn and I'm so going to need a baker. You know, for the coffee cake part."

"No way."

Vera, nodding and crying now too, assures her. "Oh yes. Way, way, way." She opens a clean page in her planning journal and writes down the business name, underlining it twice. Beneath it, she begins an outline. "Number one. Get the best coworker on the planet." Then she looks up at Brooke.

"You know what they say," Brooke tells her. "Sisters make the perfect best friends."

"Uh-huh," Vera agrees, leaning over and giving her a quick hug. "And now I know why I called you Bossy Brooke all those years when you micromanaged my life. You'll finally be a boss, of your own bakery. And okay, probably still of my life, too."

Brooke forks a hunk of cake into her mouth. "Want some?" she asks around it, her eyes sparkling as she cuts Vera a piece and slides the dish over to her.

"Yes, because I'd like to make a toast." She scoops a hunk of the cake and clinks forks with Brooke. "Coffee-cake cheers!"

"Oh, cheers to you, too!" Brooke takes another bite of her cake. "But listen, Vee. I can't just up and quit my job. Do you really think we could eventually make a go of this? Of Snowflakes and Coffee Cakes, which I love saying already."

"We'll take it one step at a time." Vera spears a piece of cake and washes it down with a long sip of hot coffee. "But we're going to need a lot more working-breakfasts in this kitchen, so keep your weekends open."

"I'm so game."

"The barn's decorated, all the inventory's out, so we can test it this week and right through to Christmas. You know Mom will want to help, so we can get her thoughts. And we'll get customer feedback, analyze sales data, check the numbers, research inventory. We can probably even commission local artists' work and stock handmade Addison ornaments, too. Oh gosh, let me list all this here." Her pen feverishly fills the page with ideas and plans, arrows and bulleted lists, underlines and numbers.

As she builds their business outline, Brooke leans close, watching. "Tom closes the office between Christmas and New Year's, and it's slow this week. Maybe I can arrange some time off to dive in."

"And I'm still writing for the newspaper here in town." Vera looks up from their expanding outline. "Plus I can pick up other freelance work to have *some* sort of income while we start all this."

Brooke stands and lifts her parka off one of the kitchen chairs. And Vera sees how she can't help herself. The excitement at having her own bakeshop in Vera's Christmas shop has her on her feet, eager to begin.

"Would you really consider it and work with me?" Vera quietly asks.

"In a heartbeat."

"I want you to talk it over with Brett first."

"That's where I'm going now. Because to be able to bake every single day? Here? Well, it's far better than me just overfeeding Brett." Brooke sits again with her coat in her lap. "But this is pretty sudden. So are *you* sure about this?"

The phone rings then and Vera gives her a look as sure as there ever was one, all while holding up a finger asking her sister to wait. She thanks the caller and tells her to check this week's *Addison Weekly* for a formal announcement, hangs up, and tells Brooke, "I'm as certain as, well, as certain as those are snowflakes out there." She nods to the kitchen window where Jingles sits.

Brooke puts on her parka and walks to the window. "Perfect timing," she says when a pickup truck pulls into Vera's driveway and begins plowing the snow. "Because

I've got so much to do now!" She watches the truck for a moment, then hurries to the table, sits and slips on her boots. "So much baking, and picking out the right coffee cake recipes for our grand opening." But something stops her, and she stands and goes back to the window, scratching Jingles' head while looking out past the big cat. "Wait, is that Derek?"

Vera moves behind her sister and looks over her shoulder. "Yes, it is." Beyond him, she sees the barn, and the fir tree outside of it still twinkling with colored lights left on from the night before, the snow falling so gently around it. And seeing it all—Derek, the brown barn, the colored Christmas lights, her sister here with her in the kitchen on a snowy morning, okay, and Jingles too—well, she's finally certain, after wondering for so long, she's certain that what she knows, without a sliver of doubt, is this: There definitely *was* a reason she stepped suddenly on her car brakes all those many months ago when this big old house rose out of a blustery winter snowstorm like a beacon, calling, calling her home.

◦≫◦

Sometimes it feels like things didn't really happen, especially since Abby's death. Derek will think of a sunrise from the morning before, or a good meal he enjoyed, or even a song on the radio, and then almost deny it because sometimes it's still hard to laugh, or feel good, as though he's being unfair to his daughter by doing so.

So when he pulls into Vera's driveway and sees the small tree outside her barn still lit up in Christmas lights, he's sure the night before really *did* happen. He has a sneaking suspicion she'll leave those lights on round-the-clock now, because how could she bring herself to shut them off? Leaving them on is a way of holding on. Of maybe turning a corner she never saw coming.

He drops the truck plow and starts clearing the deep snow accumulated in her driveway, working his way from the street, past her Dutch colonial, all the way down to the barn entrance, pushing piles of it off to the side. As he backs up to clear another section, at first he thinks it's Vera coming out the house's side door wearing a royal-blue parka with a fur-lined hood pulled up over her head and clutching a silver-and-black thermos. But when the wind blows the hood off her head, he sees it's Brooke tromping through the deep snow. He pulls up to her and idles the truck, rolling down the window.

"Hey there, Derek," Brooke says. "This is so nice of you, I can finally get my car out."

"No problem," he tells her. "It's the least I can do after all that Vera did last night."

"Oh! That reminds me." She hands him the thermos through the window. "This is for you. Vera made you coffee, just the way you like it."

He takes the thermos and glances over at the house.

"It was really nice seeing everyone gathered last night," Brooke says then.

"It amazes me every year, how Abby brings so many people together that way." He opens the thermos and pours coffee into the cup.

"I don't know how to say this, Derek, but as sad as the circumstances, Abby somehow inspires us to celebrate life. Or more to celebrate the moment, I guess."

He nods, taking a swallow of the steaming coffee.

"And we still raised a sizable donation for the Children's Hospital. Between the high school kids from the Key Club selling out all the Addison sweatshirts, and then me and my mom selling coffee cake slices, well, people were very generous. Brett will be in touch when we're ready to deliver the check in Abby's name."

"I really appreciate that."

"Any time," she says. "Well, thanks for clearing the driveway. I'm going to brush off my car and be on my way."

"Good to see you, Brooke. And say hi to Brett for me, would you?"

She waves to him and turns to leave, but then turns back. "Hey, Derek?"

"What's up?"

"Listen. It's just that … I don't know what happened between you and Vera. But she speaks so highly of you."

When she glances over her shoulder toward the house, to the kitchen window specifically, he does too. He knows Vera's inside, unsure of what to do after last night. Maybe uncertain if she pushed things with Abby a little too far by opening up the barn to everyone.

"Okay," Brooke says when she turns back to him. "I'm just going to say this, even though she'd kill me if she knew. But she misses you." She gives him a small smile. "I hope you're not mad at me for putting my nose where it doesn't belong, but heck, she's my sister. And she never meant any harm with the article she was writing, and well …" She takes a quick breath, eyeing Derek closely. "She *really* misses you, Derek."

He looks to the house again, toward the step he repaired—buried now beneath snow—to the damaged wall and stuck door and loose banister he'd fixed, to the mismatched white kitchen chairs he can picture on the other side of those walls, and toward Vera too, no doubt

174

sitting in one with a snowflake mug of coffee cupped in her hands.

"So anyway," Brooke is saying all the while. "Well, I thought you should know."

"Thanks, Brooke." He finishes the coffee he'd poured and screws the cup back on the thermos before setting it on the passenger seat beside him. "I'll talk to her. Soon."

"You promise?" Brooke asks, tipping her head as though she maybe doesn't quite believe him.

He nods with a quick laugh, turning up his hands in consent. "Hey, if it keeps me on Santa's nice list."

Brooke leans in and gives him a hug through the driver's window, then dashes off to clear her car.

Derek looks back toward Vera's house, seeing Jingles watching it all from the window. Okay, and thinking he's one darn lucky cat to have a warm place reserved in that kitchen just for him. He takes a deep breath, sits still for a minute, then puts the pickup truck in gear and finishes plowing Vera's driveway before heading over to the store to take care of that lot next.

twenty-four

V ERA DIDN'T KNOW IF SHE could get her ad in on time, but given her connections at the newspaper now, a few strings were pulled. The *Addison Weekly* is delivered every Tuesday morning. She and Jingles wait in her living room, looking out the paned window for the mail truck delivering the rolled-up paper to each and every mailbox in town.

"Okay, Jingles. Here it comes."

As soon as this week's edition is delivered, she tugs on her snow boots, throws on her red-plaid pea coat and thick scarf and hurries down her front walk to get the paper, tearing it open like a kid on Christmas morning. Her eyes scan each page while hurrying back inside where it's nice and warm.

Before taking off her coat, she lays the paper on her kitchen table. Her hands press the pages smooth because, heck, *feeling* is believing. She reads her announcement twice, then lets out a whoop. Okay, then she reads it again to *really* believe it. To be absolutely certain, she goes to her side door, opens it wide and looks out at the big brown barn, its roof still covered in fresh-fallen snow, the lights still twinkling on the outside tree. And yes she does, she gives herself a little pinch. On the arm. To be sure it's not all a dream.

Because that's what it all feels like, a wonderful dream that she's about to wake up from. She knows the old saying. If it's too good to be true, well, it probably is. And at that very moment, don't the stellar dendrites—winter's prettiest snowflakes of all—start dropping in a flurry, white stars fluttering down from the sky.

And so it can't be a dream. Because didn't she make a wish on one of these winter stars ten months ago, driving home from Brooke's wedding? Something about if ever she'd wish for a beautiful home of her own, wouldn't this be it?

She looks up toward the sky at those crystal flakes and knows that to every rule there is an exception. Including the *If something's too good to be true* rule. That exception is floating past her right now. Because any wish made on the prettiest of winter stars can *never* be too good to be true; snowflake wishes are just good enough to be perfect.

With that in mind, she pours herself a mug of coffee, sits herself down at her kitchen table and reads the ad in front of her:

Snowflakes and Coffee Cakes – A Christmas Shoppe

Grand Opening!
Wednesday, 10:00 AM

'Tis the season. The old Christmas Barn at Addison Cove is reopened for the holidays. Stop in to see the original Christmas keepsakes and ornaments kept safely

*for all these years. Your favorite one-stop shop for
Christmas nostalgia is back with beautiful, unique gifts.*

*Smile! Complimentary pictures with Jingles the
Christmas Cat available for the children.*

*Fresh coffee and pastry served daily at Addison's newest
holiday destination …*

Snowflakes and Coffee Cakes
Visit us across from Addison Cove.

∽

The next morning, Vera snuggles beneath her soft comforter at the first hint of that sound again. Oh she so doesn't need this, not on the day of her grand opening. With this cold snap going on too, it is just not the time for her furnace to act up. Maybe if she snuggles deeper beneath the blankets, the banging will stop.

But there it is again: *Four bangs, pause. Four bangs, pause.*

"Wait a doggone minute," she says while sitting up in bed. "I know that sound." She slips her feet into her snowflake slippers and shuffles over to the window, just to take a peek. After all, her furnace had been inspected, tuned up and is in tip-top shape. So only one thing can be making that sound. Or one person.

She lifts the blinds and looks outside. Yup, her suspicion is confirmed. With a glance at her alarm clock, she decides on a quick shower and blow-dries her hair while the coffee is percolating. Hopefully he won't leave in the meantime. Finally, after putting on jeans, a fitted flannel over a turtleneck and topping it all with her down vest, she pulls on her fur-lined snow boots and pours the coffee. Shouldering open the side door, she carries out two steaming mugs cupped in her snowflake mittens.

❧

He parks his pickup truck at just the right vantage point: the exact place a customer might park when arriving at Vera's barn. Then, while finishing off the steak-and-egg sandwich he brought along, he calculates precisely where a sign would be most visible to any passersby.

Only then, in all that snow, does Derek finagle a stepladder up against the barn and lift the handmade sign into place to be sure: *Snowflakes and Coffee Cakes* is deeply engraved on a distressed-silver painted slab of barnwood, the words a midnight blue, with *A Christmas Shoppe and Bakery* added in red cursive below.

And of course, the requisite winter stars dot the sign: Three snowflakes are painted in shining gold.

Satisfied, he hammers nails into the barn wall and hangs the sign beside the main entrance door into the shop; hanging on the other side of the door is the barn star he'd given Vera for her birthday. And every worry he's felt since the night of the snowstorm has fueled his preciseness, trying to get *this* right, at least, for Vera, after everything he put her through the past week.

"It's just beautiful," Vera calls out while setting their coffee cups on the hood of his pickup truck.

Derek looks over his shoulder. "I was thinking the same about you."

"Derek!" she says, waving him off and looking at the sign again.

He leans back and eyes the sign, too. It's got to be

179

perfect. A little nudge to the right adjusts its angle and does the trick. He climbs down the stepladder into the snow and watches her closely. "Do you like it?"

She tips her head and taps her mittened fingers to her chin first, then eyes him as carefully. Can she tell that he's cold even with a hat and gloves on, because he's been here contemplating the right place to hang her sign for a long time now? That he measured and re-measured three times to be absolutely sure?

"I love it," Vera says. "Where did you ever get it?"

"You've got great friends. I had a copy of the profile you wrote on Lauren Bradford and her barnwood paintings. Once I saw your business announcement, one phone call and she was right on it. I picked it up last night."

"Lauren did this?" Vera steps closer and studies the wooden sign. "She's my old beach friend from Stony Point. Huh."

"What? Is something wrong?"

"Just the opposite. It's actually amazing. Because it's like people from all walks of my life are coming together, kind of like the points of a snowflake, making everything about my decision to do this right." She looks at the sign again. "Makes it all real now, doesn't it?"

Derek shakes his head.

"No?"

"Well, maybe it makes your store real," Derek begins. "But with us? It's been real for a while now. Listen, Vera." He pulls off his gloves and shoves them into his coat pocket. "About the other day, at the cove. During the storm." He walks through the packed snow over to his truck and takes a sip of the hot coffee she'd brought out.

"That's okay," she says, following him. "You don't have to explain."

"Oh, yes I do. You said something to me there and I haven't gotten it out of my head since then." He sets the coffee down and leans against the truck. "Come here."

She smiles and walks toward him, slowly, her boots crunching on the snow.

"A little closer," he insists, reaching out and taking hold of her mittened hands. "First of all, I meant what I said just now about you being beautiful."

"Derek," she whispers, looking past him, then meeting his eyes again.

He tips his head down, talking softly to her. "And I know *you* meant what you said to me, in the middle of that blizzard."

"I did."

When he sees that her eyes tear with her words, he pulls her even closer. "And I cannot let one more minute go by without you knowing that I feel the same way."

She looks at him, silently, the tears still there.

"And you also have to know that I *am* sorry, Vera. Sorry that I didn't tell you sooner." He hooks a finger beneath her chin and tips her face up to kiss her gently. "I love you, too, sweetheart." His hands cradle her face then and he kisses her again, longer, feeling her arms wrap around his waist.

"Derek," she says into the kiss, pulling back.

He leaves a hand alongside her face, leaning his forehead to hers. "What's the matter?"

She looks away, smiling while a few tears escape, running along her cheek. He brushes one aside and she points to his sleeve, to the few perfect snowflakes covering it. "It's snowing *again*. I feel like ever since it started snowing last week, my life's just, well, my life's snowballed. But in a good way." She brushes aside another tear on her own, smiling wider now. "They're happy tears, Derek. Very happy tears."

He reaches into her down vest pocket, watching her the whole time, and pulls out a pocket magnifier he knew would be there, and hands it to her.

Vera holds the magnifier over the snowflakes on his sleeve. "Look," she whispers, nodding down toward his arm.

And he does. Silver glittering stars of crystal are sprinkled across the fabric. And he knows what those mini-magnifiers in her every coat pocket are really for— that reminder to stop and look. Because you just never know when a bit of wonder will drop into your life.

But sometimes the tricky part is holding on to that wonder. He turns then and picks up both coffee cups, handing her one and sipping from his, cupping the warm mug close. "Walk with me?" he asks. She nods and they start walking slowly through the snow toward the far side of the barn, facing Addison Cove. "You know, Vera, there's something else, too, that I wanted to tell you."

"Okay," she says cautiously.

"No, seriously. It's about my daughter. I do understand why you wanted to write her story. She has that effect on people."

They stop alongside the barn and Vera leans against its brown timber. The cove spreads out before them, the trees lining it all laced with white snow, their branches looking delicate stretching to the sky. There was a time when Derek didn't think he could ever look at the cove again, because of what his daughter went through there. But now, with Vera here, he can. He sees how life spins and turns you through storms that you think you'll never survive; and yet, you do. You just come out of the storm different than you once were. Vera gave him that—her personal snowflake perspective.

"It wasn't really that you were profiling Abby that day that upset me," Derek explains. "Something else was on my mind. About you."

"Me?"

He nods. "Writing for a Rhode Island newspaper?" He looks out at the silver water, seeing small ripples moving across it. "I figured you'd be leaving here. And seriously? It got me mad." He sips his coffee, turning finally away from the water to face Vera. "Because I thought we maybe had something between us, and then to think that you were just passing through, well, I took it all wrong."

Vera shakes her head, no. "I'm sorry I didn't explain it then. I'm not passing through. I never intended to. Addison's my *home*, and writing Abby's story was really my way to honor her, to celebrate her life and the good that comes from it."

"I know that now. And it's okay. You know. If you do write it. I don't have a problem with it. I actually love sharing Abby's memory with as many people as I can. It's how I keep her alive."

Vera reaches her mittened hand to his face needing a shave, and that's when she realizes he rushed here first thing this morning to get that sign hung before the grand opening, rushed enough to not even shave. "I didn't write the article, Derek. But Abby's such a part of this town, I want to show you what I did instead. Come see." She takes his hand and leads him around to the barn's store entrance, pulls out her keys and unlocks the red-painted door.

It never stops delighting her, walking in through that door and seeing Christmas everywhere. And to think she might be able to have this every day of her life, if Snowflakes and Coffee Cakes does well, it's a thought that makes every bit of trying worthwhile.

"I hope you'll like this," she says when she drops the keys and her coffee cup on the checkout counter. "Follow me."

Derek pulls off his hat and sets his empty coffee cup on the counter with hers. They walk through the barn to a display set on a side table beneath the loft. She reaches over and hits a switch and the glittering swan carousel begins whirring slowly around in a circle, the swans' necks arching gracefully, their motion calm and gentle as they pass the three ships in the center, three painted ships sailing at sea. On the wall behind the white swans is the tribute she made for Abby, one that includes photographs and quotes from family and friends of Derek's, and from Abby's friends too, along with a brief verse Vera wrote to one special little girl, with thoughts on love and peace and the fragility of it all.

"Vera," Derek starts to say as he takes it all in.

"Wait," she interrupts, taking his hands. "Please don't be mad."

"I'm not, not at all."

"It's just that, well, when I was a little girl, my mother would bring me to the Christmas Barn every December, and every year I searched for this swan carousel. I was so *taken* by it. And then I found it a couple weeks ago," she turns toward the barn stockroom, "back there. With all the rest of this incredible inventory. And it brought back so many memories from when I was a girl."

"It's okay, I understand."

"Wait, there's more. You see, to me, swans are all about love. They pair for life, did you know that?"

He nods slightly.

"And Abby is a part of you, always, Derek … for life. So there's that. And swans are also about transformation. You know the bit, the ugly duckling into the beautiful swan idea. And when I saw the town of Addison so transformed the other night, such that everyone's everyday life was put on hold for one day, all on account of Abby, it seemed fitting to have these swans be hers now."

Derek looks away then, and she sees it, the way his eyes fill with tears. Sad tears.

And so she whispers, *Derek*, bringing his gaze back to hers. "Mostly? Well mostly I chose these beautiful swans as a tribute to your daughter because when I think of swans, I think of the sea. And an old friend once told me, an old beach friend, that the sea, and the salt air, well … it cures what ails you."

"Vera, you are so amazing," Derek says quietly, touching her hair softly and pausing for a moment before pulling her into a long embrace. When he backs up a step and kisses her, his hands hold her face while he stands very close, making her feel so necessary.

"Hellooo!" a voice announces. "Vera?"

Vera smiles into Derek's kiss, but doesn't pull away. Instead she leans closer into him and kisses him, once, twice and a third time longer before stopping.

"Vera?" Brooke and her mother call out together.

"The gang's here," Vera whispers to Derek and he nods, letting her go as she heads toward the doorway where they stand with trays of coffee cakes.

"Hey, Derek," Brooke says. "Just the guy I need,

185

someone with big, strong arms to lift a few more trays of pastry from my car?"

"Right away." He winks at Vera as he pulls on his hat and heads out to the parking lot.

As Vera unpacks some of the coffee cakes, her mother tells her the Marches will be stopping by, and that they're thrilled at what Vera's doing with the property. "They found someone with a garage to lease, so no worries." When her mother plugs in the coffeemaker, she gives Vera a happy thumbs-up.

And suddenly the barn is transformed once again. Brooke tends to her coffee cakes, setting them up in the bakery display case they managed to get their hands on and delivered the day before. And her mother spoons coffee grounds into the commercial coffeepot, stacks cardboard cups and napkins and plates, and wipes down the counter. And Jingles somehow finds a random sleigh bell that he bats across the floor right between them all, chasing after it in a soft, fluffy blur.

Before she can even say, well, before she can say Snowflakes and Coffee Cakes, more people arrive. Brooke squeals and gives their very first customer a welcoming hug, and when she backs up a step, Vera sees that it's Amy from Wedding Wishes, here with her young daughter for a special Christmas tradition.

"I want to get a new ornament every year, a collection just for Grace." She lifts her daughter up in her arms to get a better view of the magic of the barn. "Then one day, when she has a home of her own, I'll pass along the whole collection for her own Christmas tree."

As she's talking, her friend Sara Beth, the local antiques dealer, arrives in the doorway too, stamping the snow off her boots and pulling off her hood. "Wow," she exclaims while looking up at the hundreds of gold snowflakes hanging from the ceiling beams. "What a wonderland."

And behind Sara Beth, Vera sees Derek. He hitches his head to her, motioning for her to come out. She does, and they walk side by side toward his pickup truck.

"I've got to get going, Vera."

"And I'm really glad you stopped by. The sign? It's just perfect."

"You have your friend from the beach to thank for that. So it's a sign from the sea."

She smiles, nodding. "Love it."

"Okay, good luck today." He unlocks his truck door. "You're busy."

"Santa's workshop busy, I'd say."

He opens his door, puts on his gloves, then turns back and pulls her close, giving her a kiss as the snow begins to fall again, a light dusting drifting down from the sky. "I'll call you later," he says before climbing into his truck. "We'll have dinner and talk, maybe stop at Joel's to toast your Christmas shop?"

"Sounds good."

When he starts to back out of her driveway, she motions for him to stop and as she catches up, he rolls down his window.

"One more thing," she tells him, a little breathless. "About tonight? At Joel's?"

"Does it work for you?"

"Oh yes, and here's why," she says, smiling easily. "I'll meet you under the mistletoe."

twenty-five

THE SNOW HASN'T STOPPED FALLING since the blizzard more than a week ago. It's as though that first snowfall triggered winter in the skies, keeping the heavy clouds drifting lazy over the cove, dropping sparkling white stars onto Addison this entire Christmas season. Because that's the type of snow it's been—a flurry here, a snowsquall there, a dusting of large flakes spinning down easily from above.

So what Vera thinks when she looks up at all her delicate gold snowflakes hanging from the ceiling beams in her barn is this: Those gold snowflakes are her way of bringing the beauty of snow inside her shop, and she decides not to sell them. They will be a permanent fixture now, well-suited to Snowflakes and Coffee Cakes.

Her last customer of the day left a half hour ago and now Vera begins what is becoming a daily routine, the way she walks through the store, shutting off most of the light displays and decorated trees. A few she leaves on for atmosphere: candles in the windows, the wreath on the barn door, the fir tree outside the barn. Those are set on timers to turn off later in the night, closer to midnight. This way, anyone driving past on their way to the cove, maybe taking a Christmas ride by all the grand historical homes so elegantly decorated for the holidays, or just wanting to sit by the peaceful water awhile, well, her barn and its few illuminated decorations bring a soft light to the night.

"It's Christmas Eve, and Derek will be here soon," she says to Jingles. The big cat's been watching her from a tabletop, waiting for her to slide a bell across the floor for him to chase. "Not tonight, Jingles. Everything's all cleaned up for Santa. But maybe, just maybe," she says as she rubs his ears, "he'll bring you some new bells to play with."

When she's dusting off the checkout counter, the cat jumps down and manages to find a lone silver sleigh bell in a dark corner. His paw swats it across the wooden floor and it jangles a happy melody while he chases behind it toward the entrance door. "You behave now," Vera tells him as she locks up the register drawers. "You have to be a good kitty for Santa or he won't leave you anything."

With Jingles still toying with his bell, she goes back to the storage room where she'd hung her coat earlier. It has been so busy this past week, there's hardly been time to think about Christmas Eve, and yet, here it is. Just like that. If she's learned anything these last few months, it's that life keeps coming right at you, like it or not, ready or not. "Isn't that the truth," she remarks at her own thought while gazing into her very real Christmas shop, while hearing her cat getting into mischief, while waiting to see Derek—her life branching off into so many directions, beautifully, like a stellar dendrite snowflake. And just like with those snowflakes, nearly impossible to predict exactly what it will eventually look like.

Vera slips her arms into the coat sleeves and all the while the bell ringing grows even louder, as though Jingles found a boxful of bells. They ring over and over, jingling and jangling a festive chime.

"Jingles!" she calls out while closing up the storage room. "What have you gotten yourself into?"

The bells continue to *ring-a-ling-ling* inside the dimly lit barn, rhythmically now. "Jingles?" she asks, looking toward the front entrance door. And Jingles *is* there; she sees that clear as day. He's sitting silently on the window ledge looking outside, his long tail flicking gently, with not a single bell in any close proximity to his swatting paws. In fact, he seems pretty darned mesmerized by something outside.

"What are you watching so intently? The snowflakes falling down?" Vera asks while pulling on her mittens. "Or is Derek's truck out there?"

As she nears the cat, the ringing bells get louder. "Huh, sounds like Santa's arrived early." She rushes to the window.

And the view has her stop in her tracks. Riveted. Her and Jingles both. Because making its way down her snowy driveway is a sight so unexpected: Derek drives his family's one-horse open sleigh, the reins in his hands, the sleigh bells ringing out with each trot of the prancing horse ahead of it.

"Donder."

"No, sir." Vera shifts close beside Derek as they head out of her driveway on the red-and-gold sleigh. She wears her fluffy earmuffs and mittens and okay, the biggest surprised smile, and snuggles beneath the plaid blanket he brought to keep warm while taking a Christmas Eve tour of Addison. "That is not the horse's *real* name," she insists.

"Once a year, it is," he says with a flick of the reins. "Every Christmas Eve, that's the name he answers to. Donder."

As if on cue, the horse picks up the pace, jingling the sleigh bells in a happy chime.

"First stop, the cove?" Vera asks quietly.

Derek looks at her, then nods and turns out of her driveway, steering the sleigh along the street into the cove area. They don't actually stop; instead he has the horse circle around the parking lot once, jingling its sleigh bells merrily. When they pass the dark water, she sees the way Derek looks out at it, a regretful smile on his face. And so she reaches over and takes one of his hands in hers, just for a moment, as he thinks of Abby.

They continue on then, away from the cove toward Main Street, a plume of powdery snow rising from the curved sleigh runners. They glide past the vintage bridal shop, and coffee café, and local jeweler, all closed for Christmas. Wreaths and twinkly lights decorate the dark storefronts, and people are walking into the white-steepled chapel for evening services, waving at them as they pass.

And still it snows.

"Your father must have put in a special order for this weather." Derek tugs his knit hat a little lower and turns up his coat collar. "Here, take the reins for a second."

"Me? I don't know how to drive one of these."

"It's easy. Watch." He clicks his tongue and softly lifts

the reins as the horse continues along the snowy street.

Vera takes them and gives the long leather reins a little shake, the horse answering with a friendly nicker. And if ever she's been thrilled, isn't this one of those times, steering their one-horse open sleigh on the most magical of nights. Derek opens the thermos he brought along and pours her a steaming cup of hot chocolate.

Which makes everything all the more sweet. They pass a group of carolers strolling door-to-door, bundled in thick coats and warm boots, bringing Christmas carols to the homes—homes with evergreen trees shining bright in living room windows, and balsam wreaths hung on front doors, little colored lights of red and blue and green twinkling on shrubs and snow-laden trees. Smoke curls from chimneys, and windowpanes are frosty. A white picket fence is strung with garland and red velvet bows.

And the snow still falls.

"Do you know what this feels like?" Vera asks. "Riding along these snowy streets on your beautiful sleigh, with Donder leading the way?"

Derek wraps an arm around her shoulder and pulls her closer. He kisses the side of her head, and after a moment, answers her. "No. Tell me."

Vera looks out at the dark night settling on the prettiest town she's ever known. The gold sleigh runners swish through the powdery snow, the air is brisk. "It feels like I'm in a snow globe. And someone just tipped it so that all those sweet, delicate snowflakes fall gently over everything."

"Well." Derek settles closer as they ride along. "That's not a bad place to be."

When they pass Cooper Hardware, the little tabletop Christmas tree in Derek's apartment window is aglow with its white twinkly lights. And Vera's heart is warmed by the sight.

It's a little quieter when their horse trots around the town green, sleigh bells jingling softly. Golden lamplight fills the paned windows of colonial homes and farmhouses and shingled bungalows that surround it. Families are settled in for their holiday dinners now. Porch lights shine, illuminated deer stand in a front yard, and the town's sparkling tall tree in the center of it all reaches majestically toward the midnight-blue sky.

Derek clicks to Donder and flicks the reins. As the horse prances along, leading them through the night, Vera looks up at the snowflakes. They swirl and fall from the dark sky, soft and gentle and full of wonder. Her snow globe. She leans into Derek beside her then, hooking her arm through his and feeling him kiss the top of her head as she does so.

And quietly, so quietly, she thanks her winter stars.

ENJOY MORE OF
THE WINTER NOVELS

1) Snowflakes and Coffee Cakes

2) Snow Deer and Cocoa Cheer

3) Cardinal Cabin

4) First Flurries

5) Eighteen Winters

FROM NEW YORK TIMES BESTSELLING AUTHOR

JOANNE DEMAIO

Also by Joanne DeMaio

For a complete list of books by New York Times bestselling author Joanne DeMaio, visit:

Joannedemaio.com

About the Author

JOANNE DEMAIO is a *New York Times* and *USA Today* bestselling author of contemporary fiction. She enjoys writing about friendship, family, love and choices, while setting her stories in New England towns or by the sea. Joanne lives with her family in Connecticut and is currently at work on her next novel.

For a complete list of books and for news on upcoming releases, please visit Joanne's website. She also enjoys hearing from readers on Facebook.

Author Website:
Joannedemaio.com

Facebook:
Facebook.com/JoanneDeMaioAuthor

Made in the USA
Middletown, DE
04 December 2023